LOVE WITH INTEREST

Darcy Rice

A KISMET™ Romance

METEOR PUBLISHING CORPORATION
Bensalem, Pennsylvania

To TBR
Who always reminds me that the best is yet to come.

DARCY RICE

Darcy Rice lives in San Clemente, California. Darcy loves reading, writing, and family times at the beach with one baby son and two unmanageable dogs.

ONE

The elevator doors slid open without a sound. Stephanie Robinson stepped out and walked briskly down the hall toward the heavy oak door at the end of the corridor. The heels of her navy pumps sank silently into the plush grey carpet. Although it was very early, the air conditioner was already humming, forcing cool air into the broad hallway. Before she was halfway to the door, she heard the man's angry voice coming from inside the offices of Martindale & Associates.

"I want to talk to Leo Martindale and I want to talk to him now!"

Stephanie pushed open the door. She saw an old man, dressed in a dark baggy suit, shaking a finger under the receptionist's nose. The receptionist looked ready to cry. "Where's Martindale? Off gallivanting around the world again? Who's minding the store?" The old man's raspy voice was heavy with sarcasm.

Stephanie let the door close softly behind her before she spoke. "Mr. Martindale is in the Cayman Islands on business. And as you know, Mr. Lodfuss, in his absence I 'mind the store,' as you put it." Stephanie

7

smiled her best smile. She was glad she had worn her favorite navy suit today. She'd need the extra confidence it gave her whenever she wore it. She'd dealt with Norman Lodfuss several times before, and it had never been easy. Inwardly, she prepared herself for a confrontation.

"In the case of a problem like this, I want to talk to the top man himself, not his secretary," he said, exposing yellowed teeth in a condescending smile.

Stephanie smiled back to hide her irritation, but she heard some of it in her voice anyway. "Mr. Martindale's secretary will be in at eight this morning. If you have anything to say to her, you may wait here in the lobby. If you wish to speak to the person in charge, you may join me in my office."

Stephanie strode into her office and put her briefcase on the credenza behind her desk. She sat down and waited, pretending to glance at the headlines of the newspaper on her desk. She knew Lodfuss would follow. A few moments passed, then he lurched a little unsteadily into the room and settled heavily into one of the chairs opposite Stephanie. He pulled a small rectangular piece of green paper out of his coat pocket and dropped it on the desk blotter in front of her.

Stephanie picked the paper up and examined it. It was a Martindale & Associates check, drawn on the trust account, payable to Norman Lodfuss for $25,000. The notation on the check read "Monthly interest payment, N. Lodfuss Account #26273."

"Is there a problem with your interest check, Mr. Lodfuss?" asked Stephanie. "Is there a discrepancy with the amount?"

"The amount's right, that's for sure." His bulldog face twisted with irony.

"Then what's the problem, Mr. Lodfuss?"

"It bounced."

Stephanie turned the check over. Stamped across the back in ragged red letters were the words NOT SUFFICIENT FUNDS. She felt the blood rush to her face, but when she spoke her voice was cool and professional. "That's impossible. The trust account maintains a minimum balance of $500,000 at all times. That's our standard procedure."

"Then check your procedures, missy! This check's no damn good!" Lodfuss leaned forward menacingly. Little flecks of saliva sputtered from his mouth onto the smooth surface of the desk. "I don't know what kind of an operation you're running here, but—"

"Please wait here, Mr. Lodfuss," Stephanie cut him off politely, but firmly. She stood, maintaining her composure, and walked out of her office, ignoring her secretary's curious gaze as she swept past her desk.

This was obviously a simple mistake, probably an error by one of the clerks at the bank; but why did it have to happen today, with Leo out of town—and to Norman Lodfuss, one of the firm's biggest clients? At least the old man was alone today. She'd much rather deal with him than his son, Oliver. It was far easier to handle Norman Lodfuss's angry blustering than his son's pathetic attempts at flirting with her. Stephanie shivered silently, remembering how Oliver's pale, watery eyes watched her through thick glasses.

Seconds later, she was in the controller's office. "Neal, what's the balance in the trust account?" she asked sharply,

The controller looked up from his steaming coffee with surprise. "Five hundred thousand, give or take a few thousand. Why?"

"I've got to know exactly. Pull it up on the screen."

Stephanie gestured toward the computer terminal on Neal's desk.

Neal pulled the keyboard toward him with confidence and punched in a series of commands and passwords that protected the confidential information. He asked for the balance in the trust account. The screen read:

CURRENT   BALANCE: $5,254.16

The next three hours passed in a blur.

Norman Lodfuss left the office in a fury, refusing to be placated by any attempt at explanation. His parting words were "You'll be hearing from my lawyer, missy!"

Stephanie locked the door to her office, and started systematically checking every Martindale & Associates account on her computer terminal. She reviewed every checking account, certificate of deposit, stock account, bond account, the foreign currency accounts, everything. Stephanie's back ached and her head was pounding, but that was nothing compared to the increasing feeling of panic that was filling her.

At 10:35, she leaned back in her chair to summarize her findings: Martindale & Associates, Newport Beach, one of the most respected financial services companies in California for nearly twenty-two years, was missing forty-seven million dollars of its clients' money.

Stephanie forced herself into action. She requested a detailed breakdown of the prior day's activity in one of the largest customer accounts. As the computer searched for the data, she fought back a dark cloud of isolation that threatened to descend over her. There was no one to share the overwhelming fear of the unknown future with her; no friend, no colleague. She was alone.

As the computer scrolled the information across the

screen, Stephanie's worst suspicions were confirmed. All of the account detail was missing, purged from the computer's memory. There was no record of where the funds had been transferred. All that remained was the final account balance: zero.

Stephanie placed a call to Carl Stevens, her primary contact at the bank that carried the company's operating accounts. Inwardly, she was trembling, but her voice did not betray her. Thank God the trust accounts were with another bank. There would be no way for Carl to know about the Lodfuss check.

"Carl, it's Stephanie Robinson. Keeping busy today?" She wondered if Carl could hear the undercurrent of tension behind her cheerful manner.

"Well, how's my favorite customer? Had your vile black coffee this morning?" The big man's voice boomed pleasantly through the phone. "I'm only on my third cup, so don't ask me any tough questions, okay?"

In spite of her fear, Stephanie smiled. She'd been dealing with Carl for years, and always enjoyed his bantering manner. She wished she didn't have to lie to him now. "No tough questions. Just wanted to let you know that we will probably overdraft our account this morning. That big wire transfer from Switzerland we were expecting has been delayed until tomorrow. Just the usual confusion over the different time zones."

"No problem. I'll just draw against your line of credit to cover you. Will $500,000 be enough?"

Stephanie made a quick calculation in her head. A half million would cover all the outstanding interest and withdrawal checks already issued, with some left over. Asking for more might invite some additional questions from Carl, and she didn't want to lie any more than she already had. But more important than that, as of this moment she had no idea how the advance would ever be paid back. She tried not to think of that right now.

"That should be fine. Could you wire that directly into our trust account at First National?"

"It's as good as done, Stephanie. I'm writing out the request right now. You'll have your money before you know it."

"You're a star, Carl, as always. Thanks for the help."

"Hey, no problem. Just don't spend it all in one place, alright?" Carl's hearty laugh rumbled through the line. Stephanie laughed back in response. Did it sound as forced as it felt? When she hung up the phone, her hand was shaking.

She leaned back in her chair wearily. "And Mom always said I wasn't a very good liar," she said aloud. What would Velma Robinson think of her daughter's behavior today? Stephanie remembered her mother's frequent lectures on self-reliance for a moment, then pushed the incongruous thought aside. There was no time for reminiscing. The line of credit advance would buy her some time, a day or two at the most, to decide on a course of action.

She picked up the phone and dialed Leo's private line in Grand Cayman. After many business trips, Leo had fallen in love with the island and finally bought a house there. He often stayed on a few extra days to relax before flying home. Stephanie listened to the faraway phone ring. She never called Leo when he was out of town. It was a point of pride with her. She had the authority to make any decision that might arise, and she knew that Leo trusted her completely. But this was not a normal situation.

Stephanie counted more than twenty-five rings with

no answer. Maybe Leo was already on his way home. That was it, she reassured herself. Perhaps he might even arrive today. She tried to make herself believe that, to make herself believe she wasn't alone in this dilemma, but the thought didn't comfort her.

Stephanie knew until she had more information, she must keep up the appearance of her normal routine. Nothing would be worse than to alarm her staff, who might in turn alert other clients. Norman Lodfuss would cause enough trouble by himself.

She was scheduled for her monthly update meeting at 11:00 with Sherman, the staff securities analyst, and her secretary had left a note on her desk reminding her she was meeting with an important new client in the afternoon. She jumped at the sound of a sharp rap at her door, which opened halfway. Sherman's round, bespectacled face appeared in the narrow opening.

"Sorry. I didn't mean to startle you. I'm in the small conference room whenever you're ready for me." Sherman ducked his head and disappeared. Stephanie picked up a note pad, willing her heart to slow to a normal pace. It was going to be a tough day.

It was after 4:00 when she was finally alone in her own office. She locked the door and tried calling Leo again. This time she wasn't able to get through at all. In place of the ring was a distant buzzing noise, followed by silence. She slammed down the phone in frustration.

She sat at her desk and took out a yellow legal size pad. To give her thoughts order, she often relied on the old write-down-all-the-facts method. The sensible, logical approach always served her well. She'd just put pen to paper when her secretary, Anne, buzzed through on the intercom.

"I'm sorry to disturb you, Ms. Robinson, but there's a gentleman here to see you."

Someone to see her? Not now! She only had a couple of hours at the most to figure out a plan of action. Time was running out.

"Tell him to make an appointment, Anne. I'm terribly busy. I can't see anyone else this afternoon."

"But he's very insistent. He says he must see you right now, and he won't talk to anyone else."

Stephanie thought Anne sounded flustered. That was odd. She was a good secretary, one of the best, and usually quite adept at dealing tactfully with even the most difficult visitor. Many a pushy salesman had been stymied by Anne's fierce protection of Stephanie's time and privacy.

"Who is he, Anne?"

"His name is Elliot McKeon." Anne's voice dropped to a whisper. Stephanie detected an undercurrent of stress in her voice. "I think you had better talk to him, Ms. Robinson."

The pounding ache in her head was getting worse. What else could happen today? She shut her eyes and rubbed her temples with her fingertips.

"All right, Anne, send him in." She'd make quick work of this McKeon person and send him on his way. There was no time to waste.

A moment later, there was an impatient knock on the door. Stephanie had forgotten she'd locked it. She got up, flipped the dead bolt, and opened the door.

A tall, broad shouldered man in a charcoal colored suit filled the doorway to her office. He had thick, dark hair, almost blue-black in color, cut conservatively short. His eyes were bright, steely cobalt, set deeply in his face and framed by thick, dark lashes. Stephanie found herself looking directly at the impeccable Windsor knot of his bright yellow silk tie. She was uncomfortably close to him, and quickly stepped back, but not before she caught his warm, spicy scent.

"I'm sorry, I'd forgotten I'd locked my door. What can I do for you?" At 5'8", Stephanie was not accustomed to looking up at a man. This man towered over her. His expensive suit emphasized the shape of his body, his powerful shoulders tapering down to a narrow waist. Her throat tightened as he closed the door behind him, his cool gaze never leaving her face. Stephanie felt an inexplicable shiver of fear as the door clicked shut.

"My name is Elliot McKeon. I'm with Weston Thomas Livingsgate and Wells." His thick eyebrows rose slightly, as if waiting for her to acknowledge the introduction.

Stephanie's mind raced for a moment, then made the connection. She knew that name well. Weston Thomas was a top-notch law firm, widely known and respected in California. Martindale & Associates had many clients in common with Weston Thomas. Stephanie had even worked with two members of the firm last year on establishing a living trust for one of their mutual clients. Yet, she knew without a doubt, she'd never met Elliot McKeon before this moment.

"How can I help you, Mr. McKeon?" Stephanie did her best to greet him in a professional manner, and shake off the cold chill of fear that had come over her.

"Please, sit down." She gestured toward one of the chairs opposite her desk. Her hand was shaking slightly. Damn it, she swore silently at herself. This is no time for nerves.

"I prefer to stand, Ms. Robinson." His sharp, relentless eyes swept over her body in brazen appraisal, then he turned and paced the short distance to the window overlooking the harbor below.

Stephanie walked behind her desk and settled into her leather chair. She tried to draw comfort from its warm, familiar contours, but she felt as if she was sitting on a cold concrete slab. She shifted uneasily.

He turned back from the window and faced Stephanie. Suddenly, she wished she'd remained standing. He took a single step toward her desk. Stephanie kept her face a mask of professional politeness, which she hoped concealed her growing discomfort.

His lips lifted in a small, hard smile. He seemed to enjoy keeping her waiting, savoring the moment as if it were something precious. He unbuttoned his suit coat with one hand in an easy, unconscious gesture.

"I represent Norman Lodfuss, Lodfuss Investments, Inc., and the Lodfuss Family Trust." Although he spoke rather formally, Stephanie felt an undercurrent of raw energy, of vital power and strength flowing from him. Her breath was coming quicker now. She forced herself to breathe normally.

The man continued. "I understand that the interest check received by Mr. Lodfuss from Martindale & Associates was not honored by the issuing bank. I also believe that a number of your firm's other clients will soon be in the same situation."

"This is all a simple mistake, Mr. McKeon, I can assure you . . ."

"In what way is it a mistake, Ms. Robinson?" His deep baritone took on a rough-edged quality. "The reason I am here this afternoon is to advise you that I am on my way to a meeting at Mr. Lodfuss's office of a group of Martindale & Associates' largest investors, summoned by Mr. Lodfuss. The others will be very interested in Mr. Lodfuss's story, I'm sure. The result of that meeting will be, I can assure you, a class action suit against Martindale & Associates charging fraud against the firm, Leo Martindale, and you.''

Fraud? Stephanie's poise was shaken. She was silent for a moment, then attempted to answer him, to make some reply to his accusations, but her mouth was too dry to form the words.

''I'll be in touch, Ms. Robinson.'' His eyes swept over her one more time, as if his evaluation found her wanting. He started for the door, then turned back to face her. ''One more thing, Ms. Robinson.''

Stephanie found her voice to answer.

''Yes?'' She forced herself to meet his opaque cobalt gaze straight on.

''Can you tell me where Leo Martindale is?'' His expression told Stephanie he already knew the answer to his question, but would enjoy hearing her tell him.

''He's in the Cayman Islands. He went there on business a week ago and decided to stay on a few days. He has a vacation home there.''

''I've already tried reaching him there, Ms. Robinson. There was no answer, so I had the operator check the line. That phone has been disconnected.'' He nodded, as though dismissing her, picked up his briefcase, and strode out, closing the door with a heavy thud that she felt vibrate in the pit of her stomach.

Stephanie rose unsteadily to her feet and followed him out, but she reached the lobby only in time to see the heavy oak door close smoothly and silently behind him.

Disconnected? Stephanie leaned against the doorway for support. Her head was filled with thoughts darting like nervous birds, each one startling the last one away before she could answer the one before. Where was

Leo? Why hadn't he called her if his plans had changed?

A sudden new thought flooded Stephanie's mind. What if Leo wasn't coming back? Not today; not tomorrow; not ever. Could Leo be a criminal? Was he in some remote corner of the world right now, congratulating himself on his cleverness, set for life with a new name and forty-seven million dollars of his clients' money? Was Leo thinking of her, and laughing at how innocent she had been, fresh out of college and full of hard work and ambition? She had given him all she could. Had he used her?

Stephanie rejected the idea violently. She believed she knew Leo better than anyone. He was a generous, fair, and scrupulously honest man. He had believed in her and given her a chance. He had taught her a great deal, about business and about life. No, Leo Martindale could not be a criminal. Stephanie knew that in her heart with absolute certainty. But then Stephanie knew that she had to find out who was, for her own sake as well as Leo's, wherever he was.

Elliot McKeon flipped the visor down to shield his eyes from the late afternoon sun. He turned onto Pacific Coast Highway, maneuvering the black Porsche skillfully through Newport Beach's busy traffic. In his mind, he replayed the details of his brief encounter with Stephanie Robinson. She was a real knock-out—and possibly an accomplice to a fraud operation of enormous proportion. He smiled cynically as he remembered her sexy look of outrage and disbelief when he dropped the bomb on her; a very convincing performance. Most men wouldn't see beyond those mesmerizing green eyes. But he was smarter than that; at least now, anyway.

She had certainly been surprised by his little visit; of course, that had been the idea. Elliot had learned early in his career the value of surprise. It had been a key to his success. More often than not, he was already in the middle of a new case while his opponent was still sticking the labels on his files. Being the first, the fastest, the most prepared; that's what it was all about. That's what had put him on track at thirty-four to become the youngest partner in the history of Weston Thomas. Of course, being a hot-shot attorney was light years away from the life he had envisioned for himself thirteen years ago. It hadn't been easy, but it would be worth it. Almost as good as what might have been.

Elliot stopped at the last light, where the town ended and the road became an open stretch of highway running beside the blue Pacific Ocean glittering in the November sunlight. When the light changed to green, Elliot hit the accelerator and turned his mind to his upcoming meeting at Lodfuss Investments.

TWO

The alarm clock's shrill electronic ring pierced the darkness of the bedroom. Stephanie slapped the clock into silence. The luminous numbers cast a dull red glow in the small room: 5:00 a.m.

She'd been awake for several hours, waiting for the alarm to sound and end her restless night. Now that the clock had shrieked its permission, Stephanie climbed out of bed and padded down the hall to the empty extra bedroom that held only her exercise bike and a make-shift bookcase of bricks and unfinished pine, overflow-ing with the paperback mysteries she was addicted to reading. She climbed aboard the bike and started ped-dling. As she rode, she could hear the automatic coffee maker in her tiny kitchen switch on to brew two cups. The warm smell wafted through the small condominium.

I must be even more of a creature of habit than I realized, she thought. I should be worrying about what happened at that meeting at Lodfuss's office yesterday, and what I'm going to do about it today, but here I am just like any other day of the week. She breathed deeply as her legs pumped.

In fact, the morning routine was reassuring to her. She'd been at the office until 10:00 last night, wrestling with her fears for today, examining idea after idea, and finally discarding them all as hopeless.

The memory of Elliot McKeon strode through her mind. She'd been angry that she had let him catch her off guard. Imagine if Leo had seen her like that! He had left her in charge, and who knows where he was at this moment, but Stephanie vowed she wouldn't let him down. She never had before, and she wasn't going to start now. The buck stops here, she told herself sternly, using one of Leo's favorite expressions.

She'd used her anger to keep fear at bay, but when she finally dropped into bed at home sometime after midnight, the anger was gone and the night was filled with fears both real and fantastic. When the alarm had finally sounded, she was grateful to get up.

Stephanie turned the resistance level up on the bike and kept pumping. She did thirty minutes on the bike every morning without fail, followed by a cup of black coffee and a piece of dry wheat toast. She followed the same routine since she'd bought the condo, soon after she had started at Martindale & Associates. It was a tiny place, and she hadn't done much to fix it up, but she liked it and thought it was more than big enough for one person. The small down payment had been a graduation gift from her mother.

After her shower, Stephanie could almost believe it would be just another day. She dressed quickly as usual, and negotiated the two miles to the office with a second cup of coffee perched on the dashboard. She parked in her space in the garage, right next to Leo's. She stopped with her hand on the keys and stared into the empty space where Leo's Mercedes was usually parked. The empty space jarred her back into the reality of what awaited her upstairs.

She retrieved her briefcase from the back seat, and opened the door. She locked up the car and walked briskly across the cement floor of the garage to the elevator. Okay, the buck stops here, she reminded herself, and punched the elevator call button sharply.

"Hello, hello, anybody home?" Stephanie looked up from the computer printout she was studying. The door to Stephanie's office opened slowly. A short, lumpy-looking middle-aged man in a rumpled brown suit appeared in the doorway.

"Sorry to barge in, but the receptionist was on the phone, and I saw the name on the door, so I thought, why stand on ceremony?"

The man scurried across to Stephanie's desk and offered his hand. Stephanie rose to take it. She was a good six inches taller than her visitor.

"I'm Detective Simms of the Newport Beach Police Department. I presume you're Mrs. Robinson?"

"No, miss," Stephanie said. "I mean, I'm Stephanie Robinson."

"Ah, well, that's a real shame. I mean about the Miss part. But a nice looking woman like yourself must have a lot of boyfriends, I suppose." He searched his pockets for a pen.

"How can I help you, Mr.—Detective Simms?"

"Excuse me if I was prying, Miss Robinson. I'm with the Special Fraud Unit of the Police Department. We received a complaint yesterday afternoon from one of your clients."

"Norman Lodfuss?" Stephanie ignored the hollow pocket of apprehension that was growing in her stomach.

"Yes, Lodfish, Lodfuss, something like that anyway. He expressed some, ah, let's call them concerns about your company." Simms pulled the elusive pen from his breast pocket with a small gesture of triumph. "I must lose one of these darn things every day. Now, can you tell me where Leo Martindale is today?"

Stephanie moistened her dry lips. "He is on a business trip. He was in the Cayman Islands, but I haven't been able to reach him for several days. I assume he's on his way back right now."

Simms heaved a loud sigh. "I hope he is, Miss Robinson. I really hope he is. But I don't think so. After Lodfuss called us, we checked with the airlines. Martindale's return ticket was cashed in yesterday at the airport in George Town."

The detective's words flooded her with sickening fear. Leo wasn't going to appear suddenly to come to her rescue. Not only that, it sounded as though he was in as much trouble as she was.

"What does that mean, Detective?" Stephanie's mind was racing. What kind of trouble was Leo in? What had happened to him?

Simms considered his answer. "Well, Miss Robinson, the problem as I see it is twofold." He held his two white, fleshy hands out in front of him, palms up, as if to indicate his two points.

"The first problem we've got is this," he said holding up one finger of his right hand. "According to what we've found out so far, you people seem to be missing a whole lot of your clients' money." He paused like Sherlock Holmes laying out the facts before a baffled Watson.

"Yes, obviously something terrible has happened. I thought that was where the police would get involved."

"The second problem we've got," Simms continued,

oblivious to Stephanie's comment, "Is that we can't locate Leo Martindale, and, I guess, neither can you. Pretty suspicious that the boss chooses to take an extended vacation right when this little problem occurs, don't you think, Miss Robinson?" Detective Simms smiled blandly and shook his head.

Stephanie took a deep breath. "I know what you're thinking, Detective, and frankly, you don't know Leo Martindale. He is an honest man—a good man. Why would he do something like this? He's been in this business for years! If he'd wanted to cheat people out of their money, why did he wait twenty-two years to do it? Why would he do something crazy like you're suggesting?" Stephanie heard the indignation rising in her voice. She brushed back a strand of auburn hair that had fallen down around her face, and kept her voice steady.

Detective Simms sighed and turned toward the window. The early morning sun was burning the wisps of fog off the surface of the Pacific. A lone sailboat was already on the horizon, disappearing into the distance.

"Miss Robinson, you're probably too young to know this yet, but when a man reaches a certain age, sometimes he does things—leaves his wife, quits his job, runs off with the baby-sitter—lots of what you might call crazy things." Simms turned back to Stephanie and looked at her curiously for a moment, then continued. "Leo Martindale wasn't married, was he?"

The question caught Stephanie off guard. "No. Well, he's been divorced, but I don't understand what that has to do with anything."

"Miss Robinson, it may have everything to do with our little problem today, it may have nothing to do with it. Didn't Martindale divorce his wife shortly after you came to work for him?"

Stephanie felt his eyes examining her, cataloging her.

"Yes, but that was several years ago." Her stomach tightened into a knot. "Exactly what are you implying?"

"Miss Robinson, how long have you worked for Martindale & Associates?"

"A little more than four years."

"And in that time you've done pretty well here, I understand. Leo Martindale made no secret of your abilities. He told everybody you were his number one person." Stephanie nodded, waiting for Simms to continue.

Simms cleared his throat. "You're a very attractive woman, Miss Robinson."

Stephanie's anger flared. Keep in control, she reminded herself. She felt her chin thrust out defiantly.

"I'm afraid I don't follow, Detective."

"I'm just observing, Miss Robinson. You are a very attractive, successful young woman. Leo Martindale is a sixty-year-old man, obviously instrumental to your future at this company, who divorced his wife of twenty-four years right about the time you came to work for him."

"If you're implying, Detective Simms, that my relationship with Leo Martindale has been anything but professional, I . . ."

"I'm not implying anything. Like I said, I'm just observing." Simms smiled his bland smile. "That's what we detective types do, you know." Stephanie suddenly found his expression repulsive. "You and Mr. Martindale frequently travel together, don't you?"

"Not often. If we have a presentation for a major client, I will accompany him. Most of the time I stay here when Leo travels, to run the operation." Keep calm, she told herself sternly. He's trying to shake you up. Don't say anything stupid.

"But I would imagine that Mr. Martindale prefers to have you travel with him whenever possible. A man gets lonely on the road alone." Simms rubbed his doughy hands together, each gently kneading the other. "Let's face it, Miss Robinson. Isn't it a little unusual for a woman of your age to be the executive vice president of a company the size of Martindale & Associates?"

Stephanie's outrage became more than she could bear. "I don't appreciate your sordid innuendos, Detective. Leo Martindale is an honorable man, and whether you believe it or not, I got to where I am by helping him run this business the best way I know how! So, if you think you can stroll in here and casually accuse me of sleeping my way to the top of some seamy corporate ladder, you had just better—"

"Be sure Ms. Robinson's attorney is present for any further discussion." Elliot McKeon appeared in the doorway to Stephanie's office. His brilliant gaze swept the room in split-second evaluation. He stepped across the room and put his briefcase down on Stephanie's desk. "She is not to discuss this case any further without benefit of her counsel present. Do you have any further questions, Detective—is it Simms?" Elliot leaned in slightly toward Simms. He was more than a foot taller than the detective.

"Yes, it's Simms. Newport Beach Police Department. And who might you be?" The detective's bland little smile looked like it was pasted across his face.

"My name is Elliot McKeon. I'm with Weston Thomas Livingsgate and Wells." He flipped Simms a business card. "So, if you've no further questions, Ms. Robinson and I would appreciate it if you'd leave us.

We've pressing business to attend to." His voice carried the authority of a man accustomed to being obeyed.

Simms studied Elliot with his watery eyes. "Well, I was ready for breakfast anyhow." He turned back to Stephanie and nodded politely. "Thanks for the chat, Miss Robinson. I'll be back." He scurried out of Stephanie's office, and moments later they heard the smooth, quiet swish of the door leading to the outside corridor.

Stephanie's head was swimming. She leaned against the edge of the credenza behind her desk for support. The blood that had rushed to her face during her encounter with Simms had left her feeling uncomfortably hot. She loosened her silk tie and tried to breathe more slowly. Why had she let Simms get to her like that! Her relationship with Leo had nothing to do with her success at Martindale & Associates—it had taken plenty of hard work to get to where she was now! *And where am I now?* she thought.

Elliot closed the office door and locked it. He put his hands behind his back and leaned against the door. His bright blue eyes regarded her with amused detachment. Stephanie wondered what could he possibly find funny about this situation.

"Mr. McKeon, what was all that about? You're certainly not my attorney, and I think that lying to the police—"

"Wait a minute. I didn't lie."

"But you said I shouldn't talk to him without . . ."

"That's right. Not without your attorney present. However, I never said that *I* was your attorney." Elliot's eyes lost their amused quality and turned hard. "I just didn't think that you should be exposing yourself to that kind of questioning without somebody there looking out for you. From what I saw when I walked in here just now, you've got quite a temper."

Stephanie stiffened visibly. "I don't like being judged by people who don't know me, Mr. McKeon." This man was definitely rubbing her the wrong way. "If you're here to discuss my temper, you can save yourself the trouble. I can get a lecture on that subject for the cost of a call to my mother." Stephanie sat down behind her desk and tried to regain her composure.

"I wouldn't be so flippant, Ms. Robinson." His opaque blue scrutiny pinned her like a captured butterfly. "If you're naive enough to think this isn't going to affect you, think again. And I suggest that you engage an attorney before you decide to shoot off your mouth to the police or anybody else. Frankly, I don't know yet what your role has been in this little scheme." Elliot crossed to her desk and leaned forward, his large palms flat on the smooth dark wood. His voice remained even, but Stephanie heard the rough, threatening undercurrent as he spoke.

"But I will tell you this: My client is out four million dollars."

"$4,256,898.32 to be exact, Mr. McKeon," Stephanie told him with gritty precision. She met his piercing stare defiantly.

His blue eyes narrowed. "And unless I find Leo Martindale and get some answers, you're the one who will be taking the heat." He stood up and Stephanie had to crane her head back to look at him.

Elliot paced slowly to the window. He moved with a fluid, easy grace that underscored his size. "Which brings me to the purpose of my visit." His voice was like the tearing of some thick, soft fabric.

"I need something I believe you can give me, Ms. Robinson." Stephanie felt that his eyes were looking not at her, but inside her head.

"I need Leo Martindale. And whether you realize it or not, so do you. So, if you know anything, or even suspect anything about where he might be, I'd suggest you tell me. For your own sake." Elliot placed a business card on Stephanie's desk with a deliberate, unhurried move. "Call me if you decide you want to talk about it."

Elliot extended his hand. Stephanie rose and put hers out in response, and her hand was swallowed up by his. Elliot held on to her hand until she met his eyes. Stephanie prided herself on her firm handshake, but when Elliot's eyes met hers, she felt her grip become as weak as a child's. His hand was large, his fingers long and strong. His hands were not the soft hands of a man who worked at a desk all day. The palms were rough and slightly calloused by physical activity, and his grip revealed a latent strength Stephanie could only guess at.

Stephanie felt a sharp needling sensation run up the back of her legs and continue up her spine. Elliot released her hand. "I'll be in touch, Ms. Robinson. Don't bother, I know the way out."

In a moment, he had unlocked the door, and he was gone.

Stephanie watched the closed door for a moment, then grabbed her purse and her car keys.

"A little early for lunch, isn't it?" The receptionist looked at Stephanie with concern. "You look a little flushed. Are you feeling okay?"

Stephanie tried to smile at her, but she knew it looked as forced as it felt. Her heart was pounding and she needed some air.

"Yes, Sheri, I'm fine. It's just a busy day."

"You can say that again! The phones have been

going crazy! I didn't even take my break!'' Sheri threw up her manicured hands in exasperation.

"I won't be out long. Put my calls straight through to Anne.'' Stephanie almost collided with one of the secretaries on her way out the door. Muttering a quick apology, she slipped out the door into the hall and punched the elevator call button.

In the elevator, Stephanie thought about the receptionist and Anne, and all the rest of the office staff. There was enough money in the operating account to meet today's payroll, excluding herself, and Leo, of course. She would have to let them all go this afternoon. There was no other choice.

Stephanie drove the few short blocks to the beach and parked in her favorite spot overlooking the ocean. The wind was blowing today, making the air so clear she could see the outline of Catalina Island on the horizon, looking much closer than the twenty-two miles away Stephanie knew it was. This was her special place, and she often came here to spend some time alone. She found it cleared her mind and enabled her to return to the office refreshed and ready to work again.

But Stephanie needed more than a few minutes of quiet today. She needed to sort out the thoughts and feelings that threatened to immobilize her if she couldn't bring them under control. She slipped off her pumps and put on the sneakers she kept in the car. She locked her car and headed down to the beach. She knew she looked out of place in her cashmere suit and sneakers, but she didn't care. She needed to walk.

She was alone on the beach today. Although it was clear and the sun was shining, the wind was cold; too cold for even the hardiest beach goer. The wind whipped her skirt around her legs, and tangled in her hair, so she pulled out the clips, and let the wind have its way with it, blowing the heavy auburn mane back away from her face.

It felt good to be outside. Stephanie walked briskly and concentrated on the beauty of the ocean. The water was deep blue-green today, topped with little whitecaps the wind kicked up. After a few minutes, Stephanie began to analyze her predicament. Everything had happened so quickly! Was it only yesterday she had heard Norman Lodfuss's angry voice in the lobby?

And Elliot McKeon—why had he come back? Was he convinced she was behind the fraud? She didn't know the answer, but his eyes were those of a man who was accustomed to doing whatever was necessary to find the truth. The image of the man filling the door of her office was vivid in her memory.

Stephanie turned around and headed back up the beach toward the stairs. As she got closer, she noticed a man standing on the top step. Was he watching her? The figure moved back toward her parked Audi. Who was it? Should she continue up the beach, bypassing the steps and walking further in the other direction?

Don't be paranoid, she told herself sternly, and started up the stairs. As she reached the top, she found the man sitting on the front bumper of her car eating something.

"Detective Simms! What are you doing here?" she asked, both relieved and concerned in the same instant.

Simms finished munching a carrot stick. "Hello, Miss Robinson." He emptied his brown bag into a nearby trash can, then neatly folded the bag up and put it in his coat pocket.

"My wife likes me to save 'em," he explained. "You can use one a couple of times if you're careful."

"Are you following me?" demanded Stephanie.

"Well, I wouldn't necessarily say that, Miss Robinson. Let's just say that until we get a better handle on where Leo Martindale is, we'd like to keep track of you." His manner was polite, almost apologetic. "You can understand that, right?"

"Yes, I suppose I can," Stephanie replied dryly. "To save you the trouble of tailing me, I'm on my way back to my office right now."

"It's no trouble," said Simms as he opened the door to a blue Ford sedan. "By the way, be sure and take your shoes off before you get in the car. You'll get sand everywhere." Simms smiled and pulled carefully out of his parking space.

Stephanie looked at her sneakers. They were covered with damp sand. She slipped them off and tossed them in the trunk, then unlocking the driver's side, she got in, but hesitated a few moments before starting the car. She made her decision, started the car, and headed the opposite direction that Simms had gone. Ten minutes later, she pulled into a space marked GUEST at the offices of Weston Thomas Livingsgate and Wells.

Stephanie caught a glimpse of herself in the glass door of the lobby as she pulled it open. She looked rather disheveled from the wind on the beach, so she stopped in the rest room to put herself back together. She efficiently brushed the tangles out of her shoulder-length hair, and secured it back up off her face with clips.

She checked her eyes in the mirror; yes, there were definitely traces of dark circles underneath from her restless night. Usually she considered her eyes to be her one good feature; deep emerald green, with dark, smokey centers, framed by thick, naturally dark lashes. The rest of her face Stephanie considered to be quite ordinary. Her nose was small and straight, covered with a sprinkling of freckles that spread across her high cheekbones when she'd been out in the sun. She usually didn't bother to cover them with makeup. Her teeth were straight and white—her mother had scrimped and saved for orthodontia—but she thought her jawline was a bit too strong for a woman.

Stephanie tucked in her tailored blouse, and put her jacket back on. She thought that her suits did a pretty good job of hiding how skinny her legs were, and also minimized her height a little. As an adult, she carried her height gracefully, but she remembered all too well the years of awkwardness at being the tallest girl in class.

She picked up her briefcase. "Fools rush in . . ." she said to her image in the mirror, quoting a favorite saying of her mother's. For the second time in as many days, she found herself wondering what Velma would think of this situation.

Stephanie stepped back out to the lobby. She found the elevator and punched the UP button firmly.

Elliot McKeon received her in his office, which was more than twice as big as Stephanie's. The furniture was dark, heavy walnut, professional, tastefully understated but obviously expensive. An antique legal bookcase, flanked by carefully framed diplomas, dominated one wall of the room. Through the glass she saw the metallic gleam of trophies.

Elliot greeted her with detached professional politeness that bordered on rudeness.

"Good morning, Ms. Robinson. We seem to be seeing a great deal of each other lately." His voice was impatient, as if she'd been late for an appointment.

Elliot's jacket was off, and his crisp white broadcloth shirt revealed a powerful body underneath the fabric.

He was even taller than she remembered. She wondered if his clothes were custom made for him.

"Please sit down." He motioned Stephanie to a maroon leather chair opposite his massive desk.

Stephanie's heart was pounding, but she kept a firm check on her feelings. She would not let Elliot McKeon see her nervousness. "Let me get straight to the point, Mr. McKeon. I've been thinking about what you said in my office earlier today." Stephanie felt his eyes on her, probing, evaluating. "About Leo."

Elliot said nothing, but he appeared to be listening very carefully. Stephanie felt the full force of his concentration, like a palpable beam of energy focused sharply on her.

"I want to find Leo Martindale. I know you do, too. But there is one critical difference, Mr. McKeon. You've got everything to gain and nothing to lose. If I don't find Leo, I will lose everything." Elliot shifted in his chair and waited for Stephanie to continue. Although he was still, she sensed a coiled strength in his body, as though he could move into action instantly.

"I think I can find Leo. I probably know more about him and how he thinks than anyone. The last time I talked with Leo, he was in Grand Cayman. I want to go there and find him. He hasn't dropped off the face of the earth." Stephanie's voice was calm, belying the nervousness that churned in her stomach. "I can't do anything staying here; I can't even pay the office staff. I'm dismissing them this afternoon. And the longer I wait, the less chance I have of finding him." And saving myself, she added inwardly.

"What about the police?" Elliot asked brusquely. "Do you think they are going to let their number one suspect leave the country?" His expression hardened. "Or maybe you're planning on joining Martindale for your cut of the money? Let's face it, Leo Martindale has already given them the slip. They're not going to let his accomplice go so easily.''

Stephanie was on her feet before she realized it. "Accomplice! You arrogant, self-righteous—You have no right to pass judgment on me!'' Stephanie's eyes blazed with anger.

"I'm not passing judgment, I'm trying to acquaint you with the facts.'' Elliot's voice was controlled. "This firm is in the process right now of obtaining a restraining order to keep you here.''

"Are you telling me that you're not going to let me try to find Leo?''

"No, I'm not telling you that, and if you can keep that temper of yours in check for a moment, we can discuss our options. Sit down.''

She was boiling inside, but sat down anyway. She knew her temper was a problem—always had been— but she couldn't stand by and do nothing!

"Our first option, and the one which is favored by the police department, is to forget about finding Leo Martindale and concentrate on establishing your connection to the missing funds. Due to your rather intimate association with Martindale . . .''

"My 'association,' as you put it, is a professional . . .''

"It should be fairly easy to establish your ability to effect such a crime.'' Elliot continued as though she'd never interrupted. "Motive is not a problem; forty-seven million dollars is plenty of motive for anyone. There is really only one reason to consider any other course of action.''

Elliot paused and leaned on the back of his leather chair. The muscles of his upper arms and shoulders shifted under the crisp white cotton shirt. His long fingers drummed the back of the chair in a strong, rhythmic pattern.

"And what is that reason?" asked Stephanie dryly. "Based on what you've said so far, I might as well turn myself in to the police right now, and they can lock me up and throw away the key!"

Elliot's fingers stopped their drumming. "I want to find out the truth." He stood up straight. "Maybe you are innocent. In any case, I'm positive that you didn't mastermind this scheme. I don't think you've got the nerve."

He walked around the desk and looked down at her. His blue eyes narrowed in probing examination, as if he were peering into a microscope. Stephanie felt exposed, almost naked.

"I've checked you out thoroughly, Ms. Robinson." His lips curled in a hard, confident smile. "Your past is the proverbial open book. Honor student, valedictorian, scholarship to a good college—now a hardworking, successful career woman. No hint of scandal or impropriety. You rarely even date, apparently." He raised his thick eyebrows in smug disbelief.

Stephanie felt herself blush, and silently cursed herself for her lack of control, but she stayed quiet.

"Everything about you is a little too perfect. Maybe you really are what you appear to be, maybe not. But in either case, I don't want you, I want Martindale. I don't mind telling you that if I get a conviction on whoever is behind this, it will be the most important case in this firm's history. It will most certainly ensure that I will become a partner here. If you can lead us to Martindale, I think we'll both be a lot happier. That's our second option." Elliot dropped his courtroom manner. He leaned against the edge of the desk, and crossed his arms. The muscles of his shoulders pushed against the fabric of his shirt.

"I've already talked to the police about allowing you to go to Grand Cayman."

Stephanie inhaled sharply. "What did they say?"

"The police have agreed to let you travel, with an escort, for one week. If at the end of that time, you haven't found Martindale, you will be returned to this country to face charges of fraud."

Stephanie felt the knot of tension that had lodged in her throat spreading down to her chest. She put her chin out defiantly. "I'll find Leo. Who's the escort? Simms?"

Elliot laughed shortly. "No, the police department doesn't have that kind of room in its budget. But they've agreed to appoint another person to take that responsibility. Weston Thomas has posted a sizable bond to guarantee your return at the end of the week." Elliot cocked his head slightly and permitted himself a small smile. "Looks like we'll be seeing even more of each other, Ms. Robinson."

"You?" Stephanie gasped.

Elliot put on his jacket. Moving with quick, deliberate ease, he snapped open the top drawer of his desk and pulled out his car keys. He loaded some thick files from his credenza into his briefcase and latched it shut. In only a few moments, he was holding the door to his office open, impatiently waiting for her.

"Pack light, Ms. Robinson. We haven't got much time."

THREE

Stephanie awoke with a start. How long had she been asleep? She recognized her surroundings, and her heartbeat slowly returned to normal. The bleached-blond flight attendant was pushing the heavy meal cart down the plane's aisle. She stopped next to Stephanie and locked the cart's wheels.

"Put your tray down, please." Her smile went from plastic to dazzling as she turned from Stephanie to Elliot. Stephanie followed the flight attendant's gaze. "Do you care for coffee, sir?" Elliot nodded and offered his cup, twisting slightly in his seat. Elliot's large frame didn't leave much extra room in the small space. The attendant filled his cup and passed it back with a knowing smile, then proceeded down the aisle.

Stephanie picked at the suspect meal in front of her. "What do you think this is?" she asked Elliot once the flight attendant was out of earshot. She scraped some of the greasy brown substance off the surface with her fork.

"It's chicken—I think." Elliot tried a bite. "It's not bad."

"It's not good, either." Stephanie wrinkled her nose with distaste and pushed the tray as far away from her as she could.

"Sorry, but when Weston Thomas is paying, first class isn't an option." He paused in his assault on dinner. "Aren't you going to eat anything?" Elliot was making quick work of the alleged chicken.

"No. I'll wait until I can get some real food."

"Suit yourself."

For the next few minutes, they sat in silence. Stephanie covertly watched Elliot out of the corner of her eye as she flipped through the airline magazine aimlessly. To her horror, he ate everything, including the stale roll and quivering pink Jell-O.

Stephanie couldn't restrain her curiosity. "You must live alone."

"Yes, I do. How did you know?" Elliot finished his last bite. He looked as if he might eat the tray.

"Just a guess. For one thing, you don't seem to mind this stuff too much." She gestured toward the remains of her meal. "Most people who live alone are used to some pretty makeshift meals."

Elliot shrugged. "Food's food. I don't spend much time at home, so it doesn't much matter." Elliot assumed a courtroom demeanor. "Besides, your theory doesn't hold water anyway. Just look at you. You live alone and you obviously think airline food's not good enough for you."

"No—I'm just not that hungry, I guess. I do try to make myself decent meals at home, but it seems kind of silly to go through all that effort for one person." Stephanie was flustered for a moment. She was certain she hadn't told him she lived alone; then she remembered what he'd said in the office that morning. He had checked her out thoroughly—what exactly did he mean by that? What else did he know about her? The thought made her stomach flutter strangely.

Stephanie wasn't surprised that Elliot was single; he probably considered himself too good a catch to get tied down. A man as good-looking as Elliot would have no shortage of women interested in him. Probably a nice big boost to his ego that he wouldn't want to give up by settling down with one woman. The thought irritated her for some reason that she couldn't identify.

The flight attendant appeared again to take away their trays. She efficiently cleared Stephanie's untouched food, but spent an unnecessary amount of time with Elliot. Stephanie watched with secret amusement as she fawned over him, offering coffee, drinks, a pillow. When Elliot politely told her he didn't need anything else, she bestowed another of her face-splitting smiles on him, and swished provocatively down the aisle. She stopped to whisper something to the other flight attendant who was serving the front of the cabin. They both stared back at Elliot, dissolved into girlish laughter, and disappeared into the service bay.

Stephanie smiled ironically and shook her head. The way some women behave around any attractive man, she thought, gives all women a bad reputation.

"Excuse me, I need to get to my briefcase." Elliot squeezed by her to the aisle. As he brushed by, she caught the scent she had noticed on him in the office that morning. It was a warm, spicy smell, not at all sweet, and so light, it was gone the instant he'd passed. If it was an after-shave, she didn't recognize it.

Elliot opened the overhead compartment above their seats. He reached up above his head to shuffle through the jumble of items inside. His uplifted arms made his whole torso a taut vee shape, pulling the fabric of his shirt snug against his flat abdomen. His pleated cotton slacks slipped low on his lean hips. His thickly muscled legs were only a few inches from her right arm. A slight dip of turbulence bumped the hard cords of his thighs solidly against her arm, and the heat of his muscles burned through the thin fabric of his slacks.

"There it is." Elliot pulled the briefcase out. Stephanie turned toward the window, a warm flush rising up her neck to her face. The flush spread downward as well, warming her breasts beneath her teal polo shirt.

She stood up to let him get back to his seat, and excused herself to go to the rest room. She couldn't avoid brushing up against him in the cramped area. Her breasts grazed against his rock-solid torso, and her nipples tightened from the brief contact. She hurried toward the rest room without looking back.

Elliot watched her pad quickly down the aisle. In the jeans and casual shirt she was wearing for the flight, she looked much more like a college girl than the sophisticated career woman he'd met this morning. From behind she could almost be—Elliot's chest tightened painfully at the memory Stephanie had unknowingly provoked. He pushed the memory back with a silent curse. But he knew it would return again, and again, just as it always did.

In the tiny cubicle, Stephanie took a look at herself in the mirror. Her face was a bright shade of pink. She splashed some cold water on her face. Gradually, the hot flush left, and she patted her face dry with the scratchy paper towel. She was embarrassed, and a little bit frightened by her body's unwelcome reaction to Elliot.

Yes, he was attractive. Much more than attractive. There was no denying that. But she had known attractive men before, and prided herself on not being subject to the kind of behavior that she saw in other women.

She was used to being in control, and Elliot wasn't going to change that. It was probably the tension of the situation getting to her. All emotions were basically chemical, anyway. She'd read that somewhere. Her body was getting mixed signals from her brain, that was all.

The drain in the basin made a loud sucking sound when she let the water out. She ran a brush through her hair, and considered putting on some fresh lipstick, but she couldn't find it in the jumble of objects in her purse. She had packed so quickly, God only knows what she did or didn't have with her.

That afternoon, Stephanie had faced the tough job of letting the office staff go. Final paychecks were processed and distributed. She gave the shocked men and women the only explanation she could: unforeseen business circumstances had forced a temporary closing of the office. Sadness flooded Stephanie as she broke the news. She had hired many of them herself, and she felt she'd failed them.

Only Anne seemed to understand her feelings. She hugged Stephanie and said, "Whatever it is, I know you're doing the best you can." Stephanie hugged her back, and wished fervently that she could tell Anne the truth, that she could share the horror of the situation with her. It would feel so good to have someone to share the burden with. Instead, she simply hugged her in silence.

A number of the employees were outraged and threatened to go to the Labor Board and file a grievance suit against Martindale & Associates. Stephanie understood their anger, but at this point a potential labor dispute was the least of her problems.

By the time she had left the office and driven home, she had less than an hour to pack before Elliot arrived to pick her up for the airport. The flight had left Los Angeles International at 7:00 p.m. that evening, and they were scheduled to arrive in George Town early the next morning.

Stephanie gave up on her makeup. She unlocked the door and returned to her seat.

"How long till we land?"

Elliot had his briefcase out, and appeared deeply engrossed in several thick files. He looked up. "We'll be in Miami in an hour or so. We'll make our connection to George Town from there." He returned to his work for a moment, then looked at Stephanie again, as if seeing her for the first time. "You should try to get some sleep. You look pretty tired."

"You're kidding! I thought I looked ready for the prom," Stephanie replied dryly. Elliot didn't answer. He was making notes in the margins of the papers he was reviewing. His thick, dark brows were furrowed in concentration.

Stephanie closed her eyes. She was tired, dead tired. But her mind was so full she couldn't sleep in spite of her exhaustion. What was going on back home right now? Would her friends be reading about Martindale & Associates—and about her—in the morning paper? Elliot had told her that they were trying to keep the press quiet, at least for now, but between panicked customers and angry employees, the story was sure to come out. Stephanie had a sick feeling in her stomach as she imagined her mother reading the awful story over her morning coffee. And what would the papers print? Would they draw the same conclusions about her relationship with Leo that Detective Simms had?

Well, they were right, Leo was the man in her life; the only man in her life. He'd been more than just an employer to Stephanie, more than a mentor. She thought of Leo almost as a father; he was certainly more real to her than the faceless man she had never known. Her own father had deserted Velma while she was pregnant with Stephanie. He hadn't cared enough about either one of them to stick around to even see her enter the world.

But Leo was different. He had seen something special in her that first day; a strength and a spirit that matched her intelligence.

Leo Martindale had been very impressed with Stephanie at her interview. His firm didn't usually hire entry-level people, he explained to her, but given her excellent credentials, would she consider accepting a position as his executive assistant?

"Thank you very much, Mr. Martindale, I would be delighted," she replied. On the outside, she remained the poised, professional young woman in a navy cashmere suit, sitting in the office of one of the most important men in California business. But inside, she was yelling and screaming and laughing with triumph. Would she consider it? Martindale & Associates was legendary! The firm handled the financial planning and investment management for some of California's wealthiest individuals. The rich came to these beautiful, sedate offices high above Newport Beach so that Martindale & Associates might invest their wealth, plan their tax strategies, and set up and administer the trusts and foundations that would care for their children and grandchildren long after they were gone. For twenty-two years they had been coming, and Martindale & Associates had handled their affairs with intelligence, responsibility, and discretion. Leo Martindale would accept no less than the best for his clients.

"Welcome to the firm, Miss Robinson," said Martindale as he extended his hand. Stephanie rose to clasp it firmly. She admired his iron-grey hair and tanned, leathery face. At nearly sixty, he was not a handsome man, but something about him inspired trust and respect in all who met him. Leo was a man to be reckoned with. Stephanie's green eyes met his direct blue gaze. She felt a surge of gratitude toward this man who was giving her this opportunity. She wouldn't disappoint him.

Now, more than four years later, she was accustomed to running the business during Leo's frequent business trips. Leo had been out of town for two weeks this time, in the Cayman Islands, where many of the firm's clients enjoyed the tax-free benefits of the Caribbean paradise. Leo was handling some of the larger accounts personally on this trip, as well as taking a few days off to relax at the lovely plantation-style vacation home he owned on the beach at Rum Point, Grand Cayman's secluded north side. He had offered the house to Stephanie for her use several times, but she had always declined. The one week of vacation she had taken in the last three years had been to Yuma, Arizona, where her mother now lived with her second husband.

Stephanie moved restlessly in her seat as she thought of her mother. Should she call her when they got to Grand Cayman? It would be good to hear her voice. But what could she possibly tell her about what had happened? Stephanie dismissed the idea. She was alone in this one. Totally, completely, alone.

She looked over at Elliot, still engrossed in his work. The muscles in his arm and shoulder moved slightly as he wrote. Through half-closed eyes, she watched his large hand guide the gold pen across the page. She finally dozed off, trying unsuccessfully to decipher his notes. A few minutes later, the plane touched down in Miami.

"Wake up. We only have thirty minutes to make our connection." Stephanie opened her eyes to see Elliot closing his briefcase. He looked as rested and well-pressed as when they'd left hours earlier. His eyes sparkled with excitement. *He's enjoying this!* she thought with annoyance. Her own eyes felt puffy and swollen.

"Did you sleep?" asked Stephanie.

"No. I never sleep on planes. Let's get moving." Within moments, Elliot had what little luggage they'd brought out of the overhead compartment and was heading for the forward door. He didn't offer to help Stephanie with her bag, and she struggled for a moment juggling her purse and shoulder bag. Stephanie motioned the old couple seated across the aisle to go ahead of her.

When she reached the gate at the end of the skyway, Elliot was waiting for her, impatiently pacing the small waiting area.

"Will you hurry up! We're going to miss our connection." Elliot grabbed her arm. "This isn't a vacation, you know."

Stephanie stopped short. "I'm well aware it's not a vacation." She was surprised by the strength of his grip on her. The callused palm was warm on her bare skin, and his long fingers completely encircled her upper arm. What was beneath Elliot's civilized, professional exterior? He fixed her with icy blue eyes. She stared defiantly back.

"Please take your hands off me."

Elliot released her arm. "I'm sorry." His gaze held hers for a moment. "Let's get going." He turned and walked toward the gate.

Stephanie rubbed the spot where his fingers had been. Her arm felt tender and slightly sore. She rushed to catch up with him.

They made the connection with five minutes to spare. They took their assigned seats, and didn't speak to each other until the plane was in the air. They would be landing in Grand Cayman in a little more than an hour.

"Have you ever been to the Cayman Islands before?" asked Stephanie. She decided to make an attempt at reconciliation; after all, she was counting on Elliot's cooperation.

He looked up from the file he was working on. "No. I don't have time for vacations. I suppose you've been here frequently." He returned to his work without waiting for her answer.

"No, actually, I've never been here, although I'm fairly familiar with the islands. Many of our clients have banking relationships here."

"This is a 'Tax Haven,' right? Like Switzerland?" Elliot looked as if his brain were sorting through a huge memory bank of available data.

"Yes. There are more than 500 banks here, and only about 18,000 residents between all three of the islands. Finance is big business. The country's second biggest industry, right behind tourism."

Elliot snorted. "How nice. So, all your rich clients can come on a nice tropical vacation and visit their money."

"Yes, some of them do, but for most of our clients, we make all the arrangements necessary. They don't have to travel here unless they want to. We try to make everything as easy for them as we can. After all, that's what we're being paid to do." Stephanie suddenly felt she'd been rattling on like a nervous teenager on a date. Why was she wasting her time trying to explain her business to this man?

"How convenient," Elliot said dryly. "I suppose money makes a lot of things convenient."

Stephanie bristled inwardly, but decided to ignore the unspoken innuendo in his voice. She looked out the window. Below them, she could see the crystalline blue waters of the Caribbean. Three dots of coral became visible; Grand Cayman and her two small sister islands, Cayman Brac and Little Cayman. Excitement buzzed through the plane as the other passengers sighted their destination below. Almost all were on their way for a relaxing vacation; to scuba dive, to snorkel, to lay on the beach and bake in the sun. Stephanie felt excitement, too; but the fluttering in her stomach was not the anticipation of pleasure. It was fear.

Owen Roberts Airport was new, clean, and efficient. Built to accommodate the increasing number of travellers who came every year since the mid-1950s, when the islands had been "discovered" by the world, the whole airport looked newly painted. Stephanie was surprised. She hadn't been expecting grass huts, but this still seemed far more developed than she had expected for a tiny island in the British Caribbean.

"The first thing we'll need is a car." Elliot strode off to the first of the car rental counters. Stephanie sat down on a bench with their luggage at her feet. She watched him go from one counter to the next. A few minutes later, he was back with a disgusted expression.

"What are you doing, shopping around for the best price? I'd like to get started, if you don't mind." It sounded more rude than she'd intended.

"I'm afraid price isn't the problem. There aren't any cars available. Everything they have has been reserved months in advance. There's another agency in town, but the woman said not to count on it." Elliot laughed shortly, and sat down on the bench beside her. "So far, I guess this hasn't been the best-planned trip in the world."

"I'm really sorry," said Stephanie. "Next time I steal forty-seven million dollars, I'll try to plan ahead."

Elliot laughed, a deep spontaneous sound that let some of the tension out of the moment.

"Touché, Ms. Robinson." Elliot cocked an eyebrow at her. "Let's get a cab into town."

The cab driver dropped them off in front of the car rental agency. Stephanie waited outside while Elliot went in to see what was available.

Across the street was the harbor. Stephanie could see a large cruise ship anchored. Soon, the small town would be overrun by passengers eager to spend money. She squinted in the bright morning sun. Since they'd left after dark, she'd forgotten to pack sunglasses.

Next to the agency was a small shop selling colorful T-shirts and sunscreen and other tourist items. Stephanie went in and bought a pair of cheap sunglasses. She briefly considered buying Elliot a pair, but decided against it. Let him squint, she thought.

When she came out of the shop, Elliot was waiting for her. He had taken off his coat, and was pulling off his tie. Next to him was a bright red Honda scooter.

"What is this?"

"This, Ms. Robinson, is our transportation." Elliot stuffed his tie into a pocket of his suitcase and unbuttoned the top three buttons of his shirt.

Stephanie was dumbfounded. "A scooter?"

"It's that, or depend on the bus system. Taxis are few and far between, and most of them don't want to go to the more remote areas of the island anyway." Elliot smiled sardonically. "Besides, I'm told this is what all the young tourists prefer anyway." As if in answer to his comment, two young couples buzzed by, laughing and yelling back and forth to each other.

"Where's the other one?" asked Stephanie.

"This is it."

"One scooter?! For the two of us?"

"Look, I was lucky to get this one. They had a cancellation. Let's get going." Elliot put on the yellow plastic helmet. Stephanie thought he looked ridiculous. He handed her the other one.

"If we're both riding this thing I'm driving." Stephanie strapped on her helmet. "I had a little moped in college that I rode everywhere. This can't be much different."

Elliot ignored her. "I'll drive, I had a motorcycle in college myself." Elliot climbed on and put the key into the ignition.

Stephanie suppressed a nervous laugh.

"What's so funny?"

"I'm sorry. You just don't seem much like the motorcycle type, that's all."

Elliot gunned the tiny engine in reply. "You'd be surprised, Ms. Robinson. Shall we go?"

"What about our luggage?" asked Stephanie.

"Hold on to it; we'll drop it off at the hotel. It's too early to check in anyway. Come on, let's go."

Stephanie swore softly under her breath as she balanced their two shoulder bags on her back. She hesitated as she considered for a moment if she should wrap her arms around Elliot to hold on, but decided instead on the leather strap spanning the middle of the seat.

Elliot gunned the tiny engine and turned out into the street. The momentum of the start pushed Elliot's back firmly against her breasts. She tried to scoot back, but there wasn't room, and she couldn't maneuver very well with the luggage on her back. His back was a warm, solid mass of fluid muscle, and it only took a few more bumps for her to be wedged up even more tightly against him. As he maneuvered the little scooter, she could feel the movement of his back muscles against her breasts. The hard cords of his upper thighs pressed against the insides of her legs. The warm flush she had experienced on the plane was growing within her again, but this time starting lower, just below her breastbone.

There was another sharp bump. She tried to concentrate on keeping the luggage safely on her back, but the pressure of Elliot's back, and the bumpy motion of the scooter was creating a tingling pleasure in her awakening nipples. Her face burned with embarrassment. Could Elliot feel their pebbly pressure against him? Damn, why couldn't they have gotten a car?

Elliot kept his eyes on the road. As this was a British colony, everyone drove on the left, so he tried to pay close attention to his driving. That proved to be a difficult task. The sweet aura of scent that originated in Stephanie's hair was already wreaking havoc with his concentration; it was a cross between lilac and some other darker essence he couldn't identify. He'd had to work hard to ignore it on the plane, but now with her hair blowing free and surrounding them both like a fragrant, silken cloud, it was impossible.

When they hit the first bump, and the soft mounds of her breasts pressed into him, he was hit with a wave of hot desire that nearly seared his skin. His attempt to arch forward to relieve some of the pressure only made the situation worse, as that caused her to slide forward, pushing her legs up to lock more securely around his thighs. Don't do this, he reminded himself. Don't let it happen again. It would only be worse this time. His mouth was set in a grim line of painful memories until the hotel finally came into view, and he breathed a silent sigh of relief.

The Resort Hotel Tortuga was not on the water, and

was not exactly what Stephanie thought of as a resort, but it was a mercifully brief ride from the airport. A taciturn man in a dirty white shirt deposited their luggage behind the desk and told them their rooms wouldn't be ready until after three.

"Quaint," commented Stephanie as they left the hotel.

"Seedy," countered Elliot. "Let's get going."

Stephanie was suddenly brought back to reality, her reason for being here, for Elliot being here.

"Leo's place is on the north side of the island." She studied the map from the rental company. "Here's the spot; Rum Point. There only seems to be one road."

"Should be pretty hard to get lost then."

The East Road wound around the coast, passing through the tiny serene towns of Savanna and Bodden Town. Whitewashed churches and simple houses on raised foundations stood beside the road. Where the road dipped closer to the coast, the Caribbean was visible, deeply turquoise, calm within the protective reef that surrounded the island.

The balmy air blew back Stephanie's hair as the scooter buzzed along the road. Elliot guided the scooter skillfully along the winding road. Without the burden of the luggage, Stephanie was able to use the leather strap of the seat to keep a respectable distance between the two of them.

As they approached the east end of the island, the little towns stopped and the houses became more remote. Stephanie began to feel they were closer to the real Grand Cayman now, as they left the big hotels and resorts of George Town and Seven Mile Beach behind them. Stephanie remembered that Leo had always loved the remoteness of this end of the island, and relished the fact that he was more than twenty miles from the "action" of George Town.

They followed the road around the east end to the island's north side. Leo had always said, "Go until you can't go any farther, until the road ends, at the very end of things, and that's my place, my part of the island."

The water of the North Sound came into view, and the road ended. They had reached Rum Point. Leo's place couldn't be far. They came to a stop. Elliot turned off the scooter.

"Well, where do we go from here?" Elliot looked around at the large homes, all set well apart from one another. A grove of palm trees of all different sizes heightened the feeling of seclusion. "Which one is it?"

Stephanie said nothing, but headed toward the beach. She knew Leo's place was on the water from the pictures she had seen. She walked down to the beach. The sand was soft and fine beneath her feet. She looked down the beach.

The last house on the point was white, with a porch that wrapped all the way around the house. The windows were shuttered. A wooden gangplank led down to the small dock floating in the shallow water in front of the house.

"That's it," said Stephanie. Her stomach was fluttering wildly, but she struggled to appear cool in front of Elliot. "Let's see if anyone's home."

Elliot punched the doorbell for several long moments. No answer. He knocked, then pounded on the door. Stephanie listened intently, but heard nothing except the gentle lapping of the surf. If Leo had been here, he was certainly gone now. Everything was tightly locked and shuttered, and there was sand blown up on the porch, disturbed only by their footprints.

"Looks deserted." Elliot tried to peer in the window nearest the door.

A new thought occurred to Stephanie.

"Elliot, maybe he *is* inside! Maybe he's hurt, or sick or—" She stopped, unable to complete the thought. "We've got to get inside. Can't you break down the door?"

Elliot gave her an arch glance, but said nothing. He put his shoulder to the door and shoved. The heavy door shuddered under his assault, but showed no signs of opening. He stopped for a moment, then jumped off the porch and was back to the scooter in a few quick steps.

"Fine. I'll do it then." Stephanie put her shoulder to the door and shoved with all her weight. No movement. She shoved again, and again, then backed away and kicked it.

"Ouch! Damn, that hurts!" Stephanie fought back tears of frustration, anger, and pain. She turned to Elliot. "Why don't you do something? We didn't come all this way to stand at Leo's front door?"

Elliot flipped the scooter seat back to reveal the small utility compartment beneath it. He pulled out a small black tire iron, about eight inches long.

Back on the porch, Stephanie watched him and rubbed her sore shoulder. He inserted the narrow end of the metal bar between the doorjamb at the side near the doorknob. He pulled once strongly, and the door cracked open with the sharp sound of splintering wood. The door opened inward in a slow arc. Elliot shoved the tire iron in his back pocket and gestured her in with a smug wave of his hand.

Stephanie stepped into the dim hallway. The shadows were impenetrable at first, but her eyes quickly adjusted.

Light filtered dimly into the living room through the many shuttered windows. The furniture Stephanie could make out in the dim light was casual but elegant, light rattan and wicker pieces with floral chintz fabrics. The room would be beautiful and filled with light when the shutters outside were opened. A stairway curved grace-fully up to the second level, where an open landing looked down on the entryway.

Stephanie stepped down into the living area. The air was damp and musty smelling, with another sweet-sour note that she couldn't identify. As her eyes adjusted further, Stephanie became aware that the room was a mess. Beer cans, empty rum bottles, half-eaten plates of food littered the little white wicker tables and even the floor. Her stomach churned with nausea.

"Looks like some party." Elliot joined her in the half-light of the living room. He picked up a bottle of rum from the mantle. A trail of ants had discovered the trace of sticky sweetness inside the bottle. "I take it Martindale likes to drink."

"No! Exactly the opposite; he's an alcoholic—I mean a recovering alcoholic. He hasn't had a drink for years."

Except for that one time—Stephanie remembered that disturbing night she had spent caring for Leo, after her first Christmas party at Martindale & Associates.

It had happened shortly after Leo and his wife had filed for divorce. He had fallen off the wagon at the party. Stephanie took him safely home, and cared for him through the long night. Leo told her about his dis-ease, about his marriage, about a lot of things. Steph-anie had never seen him take a drink before or ever again after that, but she'd never forgotten what she'd learned about Leo that night.

Elliot put the bottle back down for the ants to finish.

"I don't know where Martindale is, but I'll bet that wherever he is, he's on a binge."

Stephanie was silent a moment. "Come on, help me get some of these shutters open. I'm going to need some light."

FOUR

They worked in silence for several minutes. Elliot went from window to window outside, unlatching and folding back the broad, white plantation shutters. The room filled with the clean sunlight of the late morning. Stephanie pushed back the sheer white eyelet draperies and opened windows. The gentle ocean breeze filled the house and cleared out the sickly-sweet air that had been trapped inside. How long since it had been opened up like this?

Stephanie started collecting the bottles and crusty plates littering the room. She stacked them in a corner of the kitchen and put the plates in the sink. She put the stopper in the sink, and filled it with water, adding a squeeze of the pink liquid detergent she found underneath the sink.

When she emerged from the kitchen, drying her hands on a checked towel, Elliot was standing in the front door, big hands resting defiantly on lean hips. The front of his shirt was streaked with broad bands of moisture, and he had turned up his sleeves, revealing

57

muscular forearms. A bright luster of sweat glistened over his deeply tanned face and neck.

"What are you doing?" His low voice smoldered with annoyance.

"I'm looking for clues. What does it look like I'm doing?"

"It looks like you're playing house."

Stephanie felt her face grow hot. "I don't have much to go on yet, but I can tell you this: If Leo was here, he wasn't here alone. There are enough empty rum bottles to have kept an entire fraternity drunk for a month. Whoever was here was here for at least a week—and they didn't believe in eating out either, from the mess in the kitchen."

Elliot nodded. "I see. If you're finished with your analysis of our friend's housekeeping habits, I'm going upstairs to have a look around." He headed for the stairs.

Stephanie crossed her arms. "Let me know if you find forty-seven million dollars under the mattress!" She grabbed another armful of bottles and shoved the swinging door into the kitchen open with her shoulder.

"Damn!" She swore under her breath, nearly dropping the bottles. Her shoulder still hurt from her earlier assault on the front door. She added the load to the growing stack of bottles in the corner. She leaned against the counter and rubbed her tender shoulder. Damn that Elliot McKeon! She had a lot more at stake here than he did! She hadn't been so frustrated by a man since her seventh grade algebra teacher, Mr. Burns, had told her that women didn't need to understand numbers; that's why God had given them husbands.

Stephanie heard a heavy dragging sound above her. It sounded like Elliot was moving furniture in the bedrooms upstairs. Suddenly, Stephanie was furious with herself. Elliot was absolutely right—she was wasting time! What was she here for anyway?

Stephanie pushed open the back door of the kitchen. It led to a small service porch containing a washer and dryer. She opened the washer. There were mildewed clothes stuck to the agitator. She made a quick inspection of the cupboards above the washer, then opened the door leading outside.

On the porch outside, she could clearly see Elliot's path in the sand that had blown up on the wooden planks, moving from window to window. She retraced his steps, following the large footprints back around to the front door.

When she opened the door, Elliot was at the top of the stairs. "I think you'd better come up here." His voice had an ominous note that frightened her. He waited as she quickly ran up the staircase to the landing.

Stephanie followed Elliot silently into the master bedroom, Leo's bedroom. Here, on the second level, the windows were still shuttered, and Stephanie couldn't see much as her eyes adjusted from the bright sun outside to the semi-darkness of the bedroom.

The bedroom was large, decorated in a masculine style that gave it the feeling of a den or study. By the window was a maroon leather chair with a footstool. There was an open book face down on the small table next to the chair and a pipe rack. Smoking a pipe was the one vice Leo permitted himself. Stephanie had often teased him that he only did it to give himself an excuse to buy the pipes; he had an enormous collection of them, including some rare antique ones with carved ivory bowls. The bedroom smelled faintly of the tobacco that was specially blended for him at a tiny shop in Santa Barbara.

The bed was a mess. The grey silk bedspread was a twisted pile on the floor. One corner of the fitted sheet was pulled up, exposing the mattress. The pillowcase had an odd pattern—irregular dark splotches over the white surface, trailing onto the sheets. It was a moment before Stephanie realized it was blood.

Stephanie shut her eyes for a moment, and she knew instantly doing so was a mistake, for she felt the room begin to spin lazily around her. She quickly opened her eyes, Elliot reached out to her and she instinctively took hold of his arm for support. She gestured silently toward the mottled sheets. She found her voice. "Leo?" Fear made the name stick in her dry mouth.

Elliot nodded, deep in thought. He knelt by the side of the bed, cautiously searching. His large hands reached carefully under the edge of the bed.

What had happened? Stephanie wanted to take her eyes off the bed, but her gaze was held beyond her will. Dear God, was it already too late? She fought back a wave of nausea. She realized that she was thinking of Leo in the past tense, and she must not, she could not! If Leo was gone, she might as well give up now. Her only chance of saving herself was in finding him.

"Look at this." Elliot held up the frayed end of the cord from the phone on the nightstand. It had been jerked out from the wall.

Stephanie took several deep breaths. She pushed back her fears. She would not fall apart, especially not in front of Elliot.

"He wasn't murdered in his bed," Stephanie said in a detached voice. "First of all, there isn't that much blood. It doesn't look like a fatal wound. Second, Leo wasn't worth anything dead. Whoever surprised him here needed him alive, I'm sure of that.'' Stephanie felt like she was listening to someone else talking. It surely wasn't her talking so casually about the possible murder of a dear friend. She must be dreaming. Maybe she wasn't here at all. Maybe she would awake with a start and find herself on her sofa at home, wearing her light blue flannel robe, where she had dozed off watching the late, late show.

Elliot raised one dark eyebrow. "I'm going to check the rest of the house. Do you want to wait for me downstairs?" Stephanie was surprised by his gentle tone.

"No, I'm alright. Let's take a look." They headed out to the hall, staying close together.

The two guest bedrooms had been slept in, and there were a few more beer bottles scattered about the rooms, but otherwise nothing had been disturbed. The closets were empty, except in Leo's bedroom. That closet contained only a few business suits, a couple of casual shirts, and a briefcase.

The briefcase was heavy, and it was locked. "I'll get something from the kitchen to pry it open." Elliot picked up the briefcase, and was already at the bottom of the stairs when Stephanie caught up with him.

"The combination is one-two-six."

Elliot looked at her quizzically. "What?"

"It's his birthday. December sixth. He always used that if he needed a number combination for something. He said that way he wouldn't ever forget it."

Elliot laid the briefcase flat on the kitchen table and flipped the tumblers. The latches sprang open. The briefcase was stuffed full of files.

Stephanie flipped eagerly through the manila folders. "Keane, Wilson, Covell; these are the accounts he was working on when he made the trip down here." She opened one of the folders. "Just the usual client information." She quickly scanned the remaining files. "Here's the documentation on the new Caymanian bank accounts he was opening for these people."

Elliot dumped out the rest of the contents of the briefcase on the table. Pens, yellow legal pads, a calculator; the usual contents of an executive's briefcase. Nothing out of the ordinary. Stephanie checked the pockets of the briefcase, but found nothing else.

"Well, at least we know he was here, and he had enough time to open these accounts." She bit her lower lip thoughtfully. "Doesn't that mean something at least? If he had made this trip with the intention of embezzling the money, why would he have bothered to take the time to open these new customer accounts?" She studied Elliot's face for confirmation. "Right?"

Elliot glanced up briefly from his examination of the contents of Leo's briefcase. "That doesn't necessarily mean Martindale's innocent. He may have wanted to make everything look as normal as possible to avoid attention." Elliot's eyes were cool and appraising as he took a last look through the files.

Stephanie was disappointed, and disgusted with her own naiveté. What had she expected to find? A note? A map to lead them to Leo and the missing money?

Elliot closed the briefcase with a snap of frustration. "I'll check the rest of the downstairs. Too bad I don't know what it is I'm looking for." He left the kitchen, the swinging door whooshing closed behind him.

He's right, thought Stephanie to herself. We're here in Grand Cayman looking for some trace of a man who could be anywhere by now—if he isn't dead. *But that's better than sitting at home waiting to go to jail*, she reminded herself. Stephanie's mouth was set in a grim line as she started going through the kitchen cupboards.

Several hours later, Stephanie heard Elliot come back in through the front door after circling the outside of the house one more time. She was upstairs in Leo's bedroom, going over the floor on her hands and knees. She'd finally become immune to the images of blood in the room. She stopped and sat up on her knees. She was hot and dirty and tired. She lifted the heavy mass of her hair off her neck with both hands and held it up for a moment. She'd lost the clips earlier in the day that usually kept her hair swept off her face. Stephanie leaned her head back and closed her eyes for a moment. She became aware of the headache that she'd had for hours, but hadn't taken the time to acknowledge.

When she opened her eyes, Elliot was silhouetted in the doorway, looking at her intently. She jumped slightly from surprise. His large, lean body filled the door frame, and he looked even taller from her vantage point on the floor.

Elliot's shirt was unbuttoned to the middle of his chest, and Stephanie could see a thick growth of dark hair where his shirt parted. His tan cotton slacks, no longer crisply pressed, were slung low on his hips. A thin sheen of sweat glistened on his face and made damp streaks in his shirt. The sunlight from the high windows in the hall outside the bedroom illuminated him from behind, emphasizing the hard lines of his body.

"Well?" Stephanie quickly stood up to shake off the feeling of vulnerability that had come over her when he'd appeared in the door. "Have you found anything?" Her mouth was uncomfortably dry.

"No luck. We've been over every inch of this place, inside and out. If there's something we're missing, I sure as hell don't know where it is." He ran a hand through his thick hair. "Let's go back to town. If we ask around, maybe someone's seen or heard from him. Besides, I'm beat and I could use a shower."

Stephanie shook her head. "No. You can do what you like, but I'm staying. I'm not going to leave this house until I have somewhere else to look." All of a sudden, Stephanie felt uncomfortably close to Elliot. She wanted to leave the bedroom but Elliot was blocking the door.

"Look, there is nothing here to find! Don't you see that!" He sighed. "Tomorrow we'll ask around town, visit the banks he put those deposits in, and maybe we'll have something new to go on."

"I'm not going." Stephanie tried to squeeze by him, but his powerful grip on her forearm stopped her. They faced each other in the doorway.

"Look, Stephanie, I'm tired, I want a hot shower and dinner and something cold with rum in it. We've only got one scooter, so unless you plan on walking back to town, you're coming with me." Elliot's blue eyes narrowed. "Besides, you don't really have a choice anyway. The state of California says I'm your guardian—and I say we're going to the hotel."

With that, he released her arm, and walked down the hall without another word, as if expecting her to follow obediently behind him. Stephanie watched his broad back disappear down the hall and silently called him every dirty name she could remember. He was right, of course. Like it or not, she was stuck with Elliot McKeon.

Stephanie found him waiting impatiently by the red scooter. When he saw her emerge from the front door, he jumped on the scooter and started the engine. He jerked his thumb over his shoulder, gesturing for her to get on the back. Furious, but silent, Stephanie took her place on the back of the scooter. Again, she noticed how uncomfortably intimate this method of transportation was. She scooted as far back on the seat as she could without falling off, but she still felt the warmth of Elliot's body radiating out through his solid back.

The ride back to the hotel seemed shorter than the ride out to Leo's had been. The sun was setting over the deep blue waters of the Caribbean, and by the time they reached the hotel, it was getting dark. Elliot checked them both in at the hotel. The man in the dirty white shirt openly stared at Stephanie, and then gave Elliot a look filled with male significance. Stephanie realized she must be quite a sight. The scooter ride had played havoc with her hair, and her jeans and shirt were filthy from the search of the house. She snatched the key from the desk clerk's hand, and headed for her room. Elliot caught up with her a few seconds later.

"Look, I'm sorry about being so abrupt back at Martindale's place." He gave her a small hard smile. "I guess we're both under a lot of stress."

"No need to apologize," Stephanie said coolly. "After all, you are my guardian, as you put it." She slipped the key into the lock of her room.

"Why don't we get cleaned up and go for some dinner? I hear the food is great on the island." He smiled. "Besides, as your guardian, I have to be sure you're well fed."

Stephanie considered begging off and going straight to bed. But she was hungry, and even though she was exhausted from their search, she was tense and jumpy. It was unlikely she'd be able to sleep.

"Alright. I'll see you in an hour."

"Make it forty-five minutes. There's no need to

primp.'' Elliot looked at her hair with barely concealed amusement.

"Forty-five minutes, then.'' She let herself into the room and closed the door behind her.

The room was simple and sparsely furnished, but it was clean. This place is a far cry from the Holiday Inn, Stephanie thought as she kicked off her shoes. She unzipped her bag and spread the few items on the worn chenille bedspread. Her headache was still with her, and her lower back was sore now as well.·

In the bathroom, she turned on the water in the shower as hot as she could stand. She gulped down two aspirin, and got in the shower. As the steaming water flowed over her, Stephanie began to relax. She tried to let her mind become pleasantly blank as she washed her hair, pulling out the tangles with her fingers, but the image of Elliot standing in the doorway of Leo's bedroom kept intruding into her mind. She saw the hard-edged outline of his body, the way she'd seen it as she knelt on the thick rug of Leo's bedroom. She felt his cobalt eyes sweeping over her. But now he was moving toward her, and kneeling down beside her, and touching her—

Stephanie stood with her back to the soothing stream and tilted her head back, allowing the water to flow through her thick hair and down her back, trying to wash the vision from her mind. She stood without moving for several minutes, until the water began to run cold.

The white towels were surprisingly thick, and her skin tingled as she buffed herself all over. She slipped on clean panties and sat down at the vanity to comb out her damp hair. The bright sun had given her face a lightly bronzed glow, so she didn't bother with any makeup except some clear lip gloss and one quick swipe with the mascara wand.

She selected a light blue cotton jersey halter dress, perfect for the warm tropical night, but hesitated when she realized it tied behind the neck, leaving the back exposed. A quick survey of her limited wardrobe told her she didn't have anything else suitable.

A firm knock at the door interrupted her thoughts. Her heart beat faster at the sound.

"Who is it?" she stared at the door, suddenly wishing that she had put on the safety chain.

"Elliot." Stephanie felt sudden relief at the sound of his voice. She looked at her watch. Naturally, he was exactly on time.

"Just a second." She slipped quickly into the blue dress and pulled on white, low-heeled sandals. She checked herself in the mirror, then opened the door.

Elliot was shocked at the change in Stephanie. Every time he thought he was getting used to her, thought he had his feelings under control, she would change into something else. That mysterious lilac-tinged fragrance flowed out of the room with her, blended with the warm moist smell of the shower. She turned and locked the door to her room. That sexy blue dress she was wearing left her back completely bare. Her back was lightly tanned, and smooth muscles moved gracefully beneath glowing skin. How would it feel beneath his hands? The rough tips of his fingers tingled slightly.

Stephanie finished with the door, and turned to face him. Her hair was still slightly damp, and fell all the way to her shoulders. He wanted to reach out and sweep it off of her shoulders, to trace the fine line of her neck with his hand. Damn it, why did Stephanie Robinson have to be so desirable? It would have been so much easier if she'd been hard and conniving and power-drunk, the way he'd imagined her. But instead she was beautiful; and like another woman he remembered all too well, her beauty concealed a shrewd and calculating mind. The memory called forth a dull ache in his belly.

"Where are we going for dinner?" Stephanie tucked her room key into her small clutch bag.

"We'll check with the locals." Elliot gestured toward the lobby. As they walked briskly down the hall, Stephanie studied Elliot surreptitiously. He was wearing white cotton slacks and a short sleeve tropical shirt. The colors of his shirt emphasized the sharp blue of his eyes.

Stephanie waited while Elliot conferred briefly with the desk clerk. When he finished, they passed through the lobby, and hailed a taxi in front of the hotel.

The cab driver opened the door for Stephanie and motioned her in with a graceful wave. She slid over as far as she could and folded her arms over her chest. Elliot climbed in beside her.

"Where do you recommend for dinner?" Elliot leaned forward to talk to the taxi driver. "I've heard Barnacle Bill's is good."

"Is okay, man." The cab driver spoke in the soft cadences of the West Indies. Stephanie had to listen closely to be sure he was speaking English. "But too many people, too many tourists. I take you someplace better, much better, man. I take you to place is good for lovers." His teeth gleamed white in his smooth black face. "Is very good place for love." He smiled wickedly at Stephanie.

"I don't think that would be a very—"

Elliot cut her off. "But how's the food?"

The cab driver rolled his eyes in delight. "Is the

best. I take you there. You won't be sorry." He turned the cab out into the street.

"I'd rather go to Barnacle Bill's."

"Don't worry, Ms. Robinson. We're going for the food."

The food, Stephanie had to admit, smelled delicious. But she was distressed by the number of sea turtle items on the menu. "Aren't they an endangered species?"

The waiter assured her that the turtles were raised domestically in the local turtle farm, and were not taken from the sea. Still, Stephanie chose the fresh fish of the day.

The restaurant was small, only ten tables, inside a simple building on the sands of a small cove several miles east of George Town. Stephanie and Elliot were seated outside, on a rough wooden deck that raised them barely a foot above the beach. A bright moon illuminated the deep, narrow cove and the tiny white-sand beach. A grove of palms isolated the cove from the main road. The cove and the little restaurant seemed in a separate world. The cab driver was right, Stephanie thought to herself. It is a very romantic location.

Elliot poured them each a second glass of wine as they waited for dinner. They made small talk about the menu and the beauty of the tiny cove. Stephanie felt the warm, pleasant glow of the wine begin to blend with the warm breeze that caressed her bare shoulders and back. She looked at the couples sitting at the other scattered outdoor tables, talking quietly. Elliot was looking out toward the water. His strong profile was outlined in the moonlight; Stephanie thought she'd never seen quite as determined a jawline.

"So, Mr. McKeon, what do you do when you're not taking women suspected of embezzlement to dinner?

Do you ever mix with the more violent types, or do you pretty much stick to us white-collar criminals?''

Elliot smiled. Stephanie noticed how white his teeth were in his tanned face. His left front tooth had a small chip in it.

''No, this is about as dangerous as it gets. The corporate world is brutal enough as it is.'' Elliot leaned back in his chair and slowly surveyed the tiny white-sand beach. ''Quite a view, isn't it?''

''Yes, it's lovely.''

''Sometimes I feel like getting on a boat and sailing away to a place like this—for good, not just to visit. Everything sure seems simpler here.''

Stephanie felt the sharp twinge of recognition within her. This was a side of Elliot she hadn't expected to see. She nodded. ''Yes, I know the feeling. But I must be less adventurous than you are. I wouldn't even need to sail away to a faraway place like this. I could be happy right at home. I even have a new career already picked out.''

''And what, my dear Ms. Robinson, would that new career be?'' Elliot leaned forward, his strong chin cupped in one hand.

''You'll have to promise not to laugh.''

''I promise.''

''Well, you know those people you see on the beach in Newport with the sticks?''

''What are you talking about?'' Elliot looked confused. ''What sticks?''

''You know what I mean—those guys with the sticks with the nail on the end, that walk up and down the beach all day picking up papers and putting them in a sack.''

''*That's* what you would want to do? Pick up papers

on the beach?'' Elliot couldn't conceal his amazement. "You'd be bored stiff in a day!"

"No, not a day; I'd last at least a week. Beyond that, I'm not really sure. But I have to admit, on some days at the office, the idea certainly has a lot of appeal.''

Elliot threw back his head with a rich laugh Stephanie hadn't heard from him before. "You, Ms. Robinson, are full of surprises.''

The waiter arrived with their dinner, and they ate in silence for s few moments. Elliot studied Stephanie surreptitiously. He had thought he had Stephanie Robinson's number, alright. He had drawn a picture in his mind that he could live with; a picture of a driven, ambitious woman, manipulative and cunning, unafraid to do whatever was necessary to achieve her goals. Frankly, he'd agreed with the accusations that he'd overheard Detective Simms make in Stephanie's office yesterday morning. It fit perfectly with the image. He hadn't liked the detective's methods, but he'd agreed with the assumptions.

But tonight was different. The picture he had sketched in his mind didn't match the woman who sat opposite him with the soft light of the evening in her hair. Stephanie's eyes, deep emerald green, were open, honest, and vulnerable. God, how he wanted to believe those eyes. Just as he'd once believed another set of lovely eyes. That had been a mistake. He felt his gut turn icy within him. Elliot wouldn't make that mistake again.

The waiter cleared their dinner plates and poured the last of the wine from the bottle.

"Wouldn't they be shocked, if they knew," mused Stephanie, almost to herself.

"Who? If they knew what?" Elliot turned his attention back to her. He seemed to come back from somewhere far away.

"These other people." She gestured gracefully to include the other patrons. "Wouldn't they be shocked if they knew that they were dining in the same restaurant as a woman under custody? A woman suspected of using her feminine wiles to spirit away forty-seven million dollars?" Stephanie laughed delightedly. "They probably think we're just like them, happy young lovers here in paradise."

"Yes, they probably do." Elliot turned his head away from the moonlight, and Stephanie couldn't see his face clearly. "But things are not always what they appear to be." He folded his arms across his chest. "Of course, sometimes they are exactly what they appear."

"What do you mean?" The wine had made her a little sleepy, a little fuzzy. What was Elliot getting at?

"Stephanie, we're in this thing together now. Why don't we be honest with each other?" Elliot shifted in his chair, and Stephanie could see his face again. His eyes watched her closely.

"Honest? Elliot, I'm afraid I don't know what you're talking about." In spite of the warmth of the night, she felt a chill and wished she had something to put over her bare shoulders.

"Stephanie, tell me the truth about the money. Tell me what you and Martindale have done with it."

The relaxed mood of the evening was gone in an instant. Stephanie felt like Elliot had thrown cold water in her face. Elliot looked only mildly interested in the answer to his question; the same trick that she suddenly felt sure he was accustomed to using in the courtroom to catch a witness in a lie.

"What makes you think that—"

Elliot leaned forward into the circle of light cast by

the candle in the center of the table. The detached air was gone, and in its place was an cynical hardness Stephanie hadn't seen before. The bitterness of his expression shocked her into a sudden and unpleasant realization.

Elliot was not going to believe she was innocent; not tonight, not ever. She'd been stupid to let her guard down, to let herself begin to trust him. Suddenly, her quick temper rose within her. Let Elliot believe whatever he liked. It didn't matter. She could take care of herself.

Stephanie stood up so quickly she nearly knocked over her chair. She felt hot blood throbbing in her temple, but she choked back the urge to speak. She turned without another word and sidestepped the confused waiter. She walked quickly, but did not rush, to the front of the restaurant. A slightly tipsy middle-aged couple was sliding out of a cab. Stephanie smiled and gestured to the driver. The couple paid their fare and headed in for dinner, and the driver held the cab door open for Stephanie.

The driver got in and started the engine. "Where to, miss?" He eyed her discreetly in the rearview mirror.

"Rum Point, please." She smiled at his reflection in the mirror. "I'm staying at a friend's house."

FIVE

The taxicab's tail lights disappeared into the darkness. Stephanie waited by the road, listening, until she was satisfied that the only sound she heard was the gentle lapping of the waves against the dock floating in the water. No other sound disturbed the quiet of the evening.

She walked through the scattered groups of palm trees down to the beach, and continued out to the end of the point. The fine sand filtered into her sandals.

Stephanie's hot anger had frozen into icy determination. She would find Leo, and she would find him on her own. It had been stupid of her to trust Elliot McKeon, to think that he would help her. Tonight she had begun to relax, to think of him as her friend, her partner in this ordeal. It had felt so good to have someone to share her burden.

But she had been wrong. She was alone. Fine; it certainly wouldn't be the first time she had been on her own. She was responsible for herself, and to herself; Leo had taught her that.

The white house was clearly visible, glowing with a

soft opalescent light that seemed to come from the house itself, rather than from the moon above. Stephanie hesitated by the gangplank leading to the dock. Something was different about the house; something changed from her memory of the morning. She waited, unable at first to pin down exactly what was different. Then she realized what it was.

When she had first seen the house this morning, it had been shut up tight, deserted, just a shell. But tonight it looked alive. Although the house was completely dark, the exterior shutters were opened, as she and Elliot had left them this afternoon. Several of the windows were open, and the white eyelet curtains were fluttering slightly in the balmy night breeze. That seemed odd. She thought she remembered shutting them on her way out today, while Elliot had waited impatiently outside. She couldn't remember for certain.

Stephanie approached the front door with firm steps, in spite of the heavy lump of uncertainty lodged in her stomach. The front door opened with a small squeak, but little resistance this time. She stopped just inside the front door and waited for her eyes to adjust to the darkness. Gradually, she was able to see by the moonlight filtering in through the high windows above the landing. She debated turning on the lights—she had checked the power that morning and knew it was on—but hesitated. A light would be a beacon announcing her presence in the house. She decided to wait.

Stephanie knew she had to try something different this time. It was pointless to begin another search of the house the way she and Elliot had done this morning. Their search had been exhaustive and detailed, and yet had yielded nothing. She needed to see the house in a different way.

An idea flashed into her mind. She began her exploration of the house again, but this time, instead of combing the house for minute details as she and Elliot had done this morning, Stephanie looked at the house not as a puzzle, but only as a house: doors, windows, rooms. Playing detective this morning had gained nothing for her, so this time she played another role. Stephanie pretended she was a potential buyer, investigating this house as a possible vacation home. A silly game, but maybe it would help her find what she might have overlooked this morning.

She went from room to room, evaluating the floor plan, thinking of master suites, guest rooms, kitchens, bathrooms, closet space, window treatments. She wanted more storage in the kitchen. She wrinkled her nose at the smell of the stale dishes in the sink. The downstairs bath was old, and should probably have all new fixtures. The bedrooms upstairs were lovely and would have spectacular views in the daylight. The master suite was large—she scrupulously avoided looking at the blood-stained bed—and nicely laid out.

She was really disappointed, however, at the size of the linen closet in the hall. Why was it so shallow? A house of this size could really use a large, deep closet, and this one was so shallow it was practically useless.

She examined the interior of the closet. Maybe it could be enlarged. Stephanie noticed a square panel, about twelve inches square, painted a slightly different color, in the rear of the closet. What was it? A fuse box maybe? She pushed against it and up and the panel popped out.

Stephanie sucked in her breath suddenly. The light from the windows above was too dim to see in, but without a doubt the darkness behind where the panel had been continued a good distance.

She reached her hand into the dark open space. Feeling around, her hand closed around a piece of metal that felt like a latch of some kind. She fumbled with it in the darkness, slid back the metal rod, and felt the frame around the closet shift. She stepped back and pulled on the frame of the closet, which swung out like a door, the whole unit, shelves and all, to reveal an opening leading into a pitch black space. A block of cool, dry air moved out from the space and flowed over Stephanie.

Stephanie groped around on the right side of the smooth wall inside the space. Her fingers found the switch. She flicked it on, and was momentarily blinded by the brightness of the bare bulb above.

The room was about eight feet deep, configured like a large walk-in closet. Both right and left walls were covered with floor-to-ceiling wine racks, handsome dark mahogany crisscrossing and creating a diamond pattern. Most of the diamonds were stacked with bottles of wine. The bright light of the bare bulb overhead glistened brightly on the colorful bottles. Leo's wine cellar was extensive and apparently still intact from his drinking days.

At the end of the space was a small table, with a chair facing the back wall. On the table was a small computer. Its dark screen stared back at Stephanie like a large, blind eye. The keyboard sat propped up, as if waiting for someone to resume his work.

The computer was a familiar sight to Stephanie. In fact, it was identical to the machine she had spent so many hours working with in her office at Martindale & Associates. She flipped the switch on its side and it hummed into life, beeping through its self-test procedures. To the right of the computer was an external modem. With the modem and a phone line, an educated user could communicate with almost any other computer system in the world, provided that person knew enough about the computer he was calling at the other end.

Stephanie looked around for a phone line, but found nothing. She quickly checked the phone in the adjacent guest room. The cord connecting the phone to the wall had been replaced with one long enough to easily reach out the door and into the wine cellar. Stephanie unplugged the extension and pulled the cord behind her into the cellar and plugged the end into the modem.

Stephanie felt a bizarre exhilaration: This was where it had happened! From this tiny room, thousands of miles away, someone had access to the same information and the same functions that she had in her office in Newport Beach! Here, wedged between hundreds of bottles of vintage wines, someone had electronically manipulated millions of dollars out of Martindale & Associates accounts and into some secret Swiss or Caymanian bank account. In those banks, Stephanie knew, discretion was a time-honored tradition. The identity of their customers was so closely guarded that even those bank officers who handled the accounts knew them only by coded number; and the source of the customers' funds was no one's business.

The computer screen glowed green, waiting. Stephanie sat down in the chair facing the softly humming machine. She picked up the keyboard, stretching out the coiled cord connecting it to the computer, and placed it across her knees. Her fingers were poised above the keyboard when she heard it.

Stephanie recognized the short, sharp squeak as a sound she knew, although it was a moment before she was able to place it. She felt an instant of confusion before her mind ferreted out the memory, and she recognized the sound. It was the small squeak of protest the front door made each time it opened.

Stephanie slipped to the switch by the wall and turned out the overhead light. The door to the wine cellar was ajar about eight inches. She could see the open door clearly in the greenish glow of the computer's screen. She quickly moved to the back of the room and turned the screen down to black. It was only two steps back to the door. From downstairs there was a loud splintering sound, followed by a string of unintelligible swearing. Stephanie knelt by the false door and pulled it closed. She held it closed, afraid to try to find the latch in the pitch-black darkness of the wine cellar. She became aware of a growing tightness in her chest. A trickle of sweat ran down the center of her bare back.

Straining to hear, Stephanie leaned up close to the door. She heard another bump from below, and then nothing. She heard another sound, and realized it was her own breathing. She held her breath for a moment.

Was there someone on the stairs? Or was it the pounding of her heart? She shifted slightly, sending needles of tingling pain through her tight thigh muscles. Her right leg had fallen asleep. She bit her lip to keep back a moan of discomfort.

The door jerked open suddenly. Stephanie lost her balance, and fell into the darkness of the hall. She was on her hands and knees, the smooth, polished surface of the wooden floor cold beneath her palms. A large rough hand grabbed her wrist. Her arm was twisted behind her back and a sharp ripping pain shot through her shoulder.

Her scream was stopped by a filthy hand over her mouth. A sinewy arm pinned her against a sweaty, reeking chest. Stephanie was blinded by the bright beam of a large flashlight in her face.

"Well, ain't you a nice one." The voice had a rough Cockney twang, and came from somewhere behind the searing circle of light that filled her vision. "Be careful, Ben. The boss said she was a sly bit." Her captor squeezed her more tightly. The rough, sweaty fabric of his shirt rubbed against the bare skin of her back.

As Stephanie's eyes adjusted, she could make out the man holding the light. He was a tall, heavy man, with dirty, curly red hair, and a scruffy beard the same color. All she could see of the other man who held her pinned was the thumb of the black hand he held over her mouth.

"Nice dress." The red-haired man spoke again. He swept the beam of the flashlight over Stephanie's body lasciviously. "The boss won't believe our luck, Ben, that she come right to us. I thought we'd have a bit of a chase, but she made it easy." He laughed, a dark, guttural sound that sickened her.

The red-haired man let the beam come to rest on the triangle of bare skin between her breasts. "I see why he wants her for himself." He reached out and traced the outline of the triangle with a dirty finger.

Stephanie squirmed in revulsion. The red-haired man laughed crudely, took a step back, and suddenly dropped the flashlight. A dark object hit the back of his skull with a sickening thud. He slumped to his knees.

The man holding Stephanie released her. She fell to the floor and rolled into the open doorway of the wine cellar. The flashlight was spinning in a slow, drunken circle on the polished floor, and in its erratic beam she saw Elliot bring down the tire iron on the Caribbean's head.

The Caribbean deflected the blow to his shoulder, and smashed Elliot broadside on his temple with his other hand. In the nightmarish beam of the spinning flashlight, Stephanie saw the red-haired man dive for Elliot's knees.

"Elliot!" The flashlight, kicked by someone's foot, spun down the hall and bounced down the stairs. Stephanie's scream was swallowed up in the velvet darkness of the night. Straining in the darkness, she could see nothing from her spot in the doorway of the wine cellar, but the sickening sound of the struggle of three men in the darkness seemed to be moving away from her, in the direction of the staircase.

The shattering crack of a shot split the air, as the brief spear of bright orange light flashed from the barrel of an unseen gun and lit the scene like a paparazzo's flash. The flash exploded again, and in its split second of brilliance Stephanie saw the look of disbelief on Elliot's face as he fell backward down the stairs.

SIX

Stephanie covered her ears, but she couldn't shut out the scraping sound of Elliot's body rolling down the stairs. It seemed to take forever for it to reach the bottom. When it came to rest with a terrible thud, Stephanie felt the sound echo in the pit of her stomach. She shut her eyes tightly, but the image of Elliot's face hung before her like a specter, his mouth a dark wide circle of surprise.

The rough sound of angry cursing brought Stephanie back to reality with a jolt. She opened her eyes wide, peering into the darkness. She gripped the doorway tightly to keep herself upright on her scraped knees. Where were her attackers?

"Come on, Ben!" The Cockney was only a few steps down the hall. She held her breath as the sound of the men's voices moved downstairs. She strained to hear what they were saying, but between the two harshly different dialects, she couldn't make sense of the words. In a few seconds, they would be back for her, and this time she was alone. Elliot would not be there for her.

Stephanie shivered in the darkness. A feeling of bitter anger at herself rose in her throat, stronger than her own fear. This had all happened because of her. Why had she come back to Leo's place alone? Somehow, she had to get to Elliot.

The front door slammed distantly. Stephanie waited, straining to hear a sound, a voice. Had they left? Or were they still in the room below? She couldn't be sure.

Stephanie got to her feet, listening intently, fighting the fog clouding her mind. Had the two men forgotten her in the confusion? Or were they coming back? It didn't matter. Let them come back. She didn't care now. She had to find Elliot. She waited in the open doorway of the wine cellar as her eyes adjusted to the darkness. She was growing numb, as if she'd been to the dentist and the novocaine was somehow spreading throughout her entire body.

A low moaning sound came from somewhere downstairs. Someone was calling her name from downstairs! She stepped out into the hall. Dear God, Elliot must be alive!

"Stephanie . . ."

Stephanie commanded her legs to move, to hurry downstairs, but she felt like she was slogging through waist-deep mud.

She finally reached the bottom. Elliot was in a crumpled pile on the floor, illuminated in a shaft of moonlight from the high windows of the landing. A sticky pool was spreading out on the smooth, polished floor beneath his right temple. Stephanie knelt down beside him and laid her hand softly against his chest. She felt it move sharply beneath her palm.

He was alive. Relief rushed through Stephanie like a burst of adrenaline. Alive! She tilted her face back into the shaft of light that encircled them. Tears of relief burned down her cheeks.

Stephanie carefully stretched Elliot out on the floor. His breathing was shallow and ragged, but regular. She ran her hands over his arms, chest, legs, and thighs, but found no sign of a gunshot wound. The shot must have missed its mark in the darkness and confusion. She rolled up the small rug that had been at the foot of the stairs, and gently propped up his head and shoulders.

Stephanie went to the kitchen and filled a bowl with cool water and found a clean towel in a drawer. She knelt beside him and sponged off his face. There was a deep cut on Elliot's temple, just below his hairline. She cleaned away the already dried blood.

As Stephanie worked, a strange feeling of unreality descended on her, a calm she did not understand, but accepted gratefully. She studiously avoided thinking about the events of the last few minutes. She concentrated only on Elliot, on the reality of his living body stretched out before her.

Stephanie carefully cleaned the layer of grime off his face, studying his features as she worked. His jaw, broad and determined, was relieved by a small dimple in his chin. His nose was large and very straight. There was a small cut on one of his high cheekbones. As she wiped his mouth, his full lips parted slightly with breath, and she saw the small chip in his left front tooth that she'd noticed at dinner. His dark hair was thick, and somewhat unruly in spite of its conservative cut. Under her fingers, it felt thick without being coarse. She combed it back off his forehead with her fingers, smoothing it carefully over his head. Stephanie's searching fingers found a large, raised bump on the left side of his head. She sucked in her breath as she touched the swelling. Where else might he be hurt?

Elliot's breathing became more deep and even. Stephanie unbuttoned his torn shirt, searching grimly for further injuries. His torso was hard and muscular, with a cloud of dark curly hair covering the breadth of his chest, becoming lighter over the taut quadrants of his abdomen. A purplish bruise was forming at the base of his rib cage on his right side. She carefully laid her hand over the darkening spot. His ribs felt intact beneath her searching fingers. Only a bruise, but his skin burned hot and feverish to the touch.

Stephanie dipped the towel into the water and began to wipe the sweat and dirt from his neck as she attempted to cool the fever away. Her fingers lingered over the hardness of his Adam's apple. She pulled the shirt back off his shoulders, and gently sponged all around the base of his powerful neck where it spread out to meet his rock-hard shoulders.

Elliot's chest rose and fell with a slow, relaxed rhythm. Stephanie could feel the hardness of his chest through the damp cloth. A few droplets of water shimmered on his smooth bronze skin. Her hand continued down to his flat, firm stomach. She concentrated intently on her work, her hand moving in a circular pattern down to the waistband of the white cotton trousers.

Stephanie shuddered when she saw the bright red blood soaking through the left leg of Elliot's trousers below the knee. Without hesitation, Stephanie quickly unbuttoned his trousers and drew them off in one smooth motion. He was bleeding from a long, ragged slash on his calf. Stephanie's heart pounded at the amount of blood staining his leg, but when she cleaned it away, she was relieved to discover the cut was ugly looking, but not deep. She was able to stop the bleeding with the gentle pressure of her hand. When she was satisfied that the cut was indeed superficial, and that she'd effectively stopped the bleeding, she sat back on her heels and looked at him.

His body was truly magnificent. Clad only in white cotton briefs that did little to conceal the essence of his masculinity, he looked as if he might have just kicked the blankets off his bed on a warm summer night. Stephanie wondered, with an odd pang, how many women had seen him in just that way.

She had originally guessed him at about 6′ 2″, but now, stretched out before her like this, she revised her estimate to 6′ 4″. Unlike some men of his size, Elliot's whole body, even in repose, was supremely well proportioned, every aspect of his physique matched perfectly to the whole.

His lower body, like his torso, was lean and defined. His thighs were thick, and the cords of his long muscles moved just below the skin. His feet were large and powerful with blunt, square toes. The only flaw was a large thick scar that encircled his right knee, and extended partway up his thigh.

Elliot shifted, and murmured something Stephanie couldn't understand. She watched his face intently. She took his large, rough hand in her own.

"Elliot? Elliot, can you hear me?" She leaned over him. She could see his eyes moving beneath their lids. His eyes opened in a half-mast, sleepy expression.

"What happened? Where are we?" His voice was thick, and sounded like he was coming out of a very deep sleep.

"Shh, Elliot, it's okay." She wiped his forehead with the damp cloth. "We're at Leo's. You've had a bad fall.'' Her fingers interwove with his thick hair. ''Don't try to move just yet.''

Elliot looked perplexed. He reached up and touched her cheek very softly, tracing the outline with a roughened fingertip. ''But you're alright?'' Stephanie's throat tightened at the sincere concern in his cobalt eyes. She covered his hand with her own and pressed it to her cheek.

''Yes, I'm alright.'' Even in his disoriented state, his first thought was for her. Tears welled up behind her eyes at the unfamiliar feeling of being watched over.

''That's good.'' Elliot reached up and put his other hand on her other cheek, cradling her face gently in his big hands. Wordlessly, he drew her down to kiss him. His lips were gentle, reassuring, and Stephanie gratefully received comfort from them.

He pulled her down against him, his hand in the middle of her bare back pressing her firmly against the hardness of his chest. His lips tasted her, savoring her like something rare and precious. His hands were in her hair now, pressing her mouth more fully into his. His tongue moved gently over her lips, delicately caressing them, not intruding, not demanding, but willing to wait.

Relief washed through Stephanie like a cleansing stream. Elliot was alive, and he was here with her. She was safe. She was in his arms. She would survive.

Elliot gently tipped back her head, and tasted the soft skin of her neck with light, feathery kisses. Stephanie opened her hands flat against his bare chest, spreading her fingers over the warm solid muscles. She marvelled at how they could be both hard and fluid, shifting beneath his smooth, bronzed skin.

Elliot returned to her mouth, and this time her lips parted to take him inside her. His tongue gently entered her, exploring her mouth with pleasure. She responded, timid at first, then eager, anxious to taste and explore his lips, mouth, tongue. Her hands were eagerly wandering over his torso, her fingers feeling the muscles move as he pressed her more tightly to him.

Gently, Elliot broke the kiss. He looked at Stephanie with clarity. His eyes brightened suddenly, as if things were coming into focus. He sat up slightly and surveyed the room as if seeing it for the first time. A wave of pain seemed to sweep over him and he laid back down, gently lowering his head to the floor.

"Lock the back door." His blue gaze was suddenly hard and sharp, his voice unexpectedly cool and precise.

"What?" Elliot's abrupt change in manner made Stephanie feel suddenly disoriented, as if it were her, not Elliot, that had received a solid blow to the head.

"Lock the back door—the one in the kitchen. That's how I got in. It was open." He closed his eyes for a moment. "And don't turn on any lights! We don't want to give those two goons any warning if they come back here."

Come back? She hadn't had time to consider that possibility since she'd discovered Elliot was alive. Stephanie started to say something, but the sudden note of authority in Elliot's voice left no room for discussion.

The moon was higher in the night sky now, and cast a bright glow through the house's many windows. She pushed open the swinging door to the kitchen.

She found the back door slightly ajar. Outside by a clump of palms, she could make out the outline of their scooter. What would happen if Elliot hadn't shown up when he did? Who were those two men? Were they simply thieves, looking for an easy haul? No; she remembered with terrifying accuracy what the Cockney had said. "The boss wants her for himself." They had been looking for her.

She shivered, in spite of the warmth of the night, and closed the door. She found the deadbolt and turned it with a soft click.

When she returned to the living room, Elliot was standing by the stairs. He was holding on to the banister for support.

"Put one of these chairs under the doorknob." He gestured toward the front door unsteadily. Stephanie took the most sturdy appearing one and wedged the back solidly beneath the doorknob.

"That's not going to keep anyone out, but the lock's broken, and I don't like the idea of being walked in on without warning." Elliot's knees buckled, and he grasped the banister more firmly. He looked as if he might faint.

"Elliot, I think you'd better sit down." She took his arm, and led him to the long sofa facing the fireplace. He sat down without protest.

"Go upstairs. Find the tire iron. I think I dropped it when I fell." Elliot leaned his head back against the sofa and closed his eyes.

Stephanie went quickly up the stairs, holding on to the railing, but taking the steps two at a time. The comforting feeling of calm had disappeared, and she was now beginning to feel the effects of her ordeal. By the time she reached the landing, her knees were weak, and a sick feeling was growing in her stomach. She searched in the dim light for the tire iron.

She found it in a corner. When she picked it up, she felt something sticky on it, and dropped it in disgust. Even in the darkness she knew it was blood. She forced herself to pick it up again.

Somehow, she made her way back downstairs. Elliot was standing by the fireplace. He seemed to be deep in thought. He had pulled his trousers back on, but his shirt was open, his chest a hard outline in the moonlight. Stephanie crossed to him and handed him the tire iron. He took it wordlessly and shoved it in his back pocket, as casually as a pocket comb. He put his hands on her shoulders with a gentleness she had not seen in him before. He studied her face intently. Stephanie felt the same sensation of examination she had felt the first time she had seen Elliot McKeon in her office. That morning seemed a very long time ago now. But this time his probing gaze seemed to be searching for something different than before.

Elliot shifted a little unsteadily, as though he felt faint. Although he instantly recovered, Stephanie sensed his tremendous fatigue.

"Elliot, I think you'd better sit down. You've had a bad fall, and you need to take it easy." She put her hands on his broad shoulders and gently pushed him down on the couch. He sat down heavily. His eyes were beginning to betray his need for rest.

"Elliot, you stretch out here and go to sleep."

Without protest, Elliot swung his long legs up onto the couch. Stephanie brushed back the hair from his forehead. She was relieved to find the fever she had felt earlier was gone.

"What about you?" He grabbed at her hand. "There's room for two." Stephanie reluctantly pulled her hand away.

"I'll sit up here and keep watch." She gestured toward a comfortable looking armchair. She stood over Elliot, ready to argue, but that wasn't necessary. He had already closed his eyes. Stephanie waited until his breathing was regular, then went to the chair opposite him and sat down.

She was tired, but she knew she wouldn't sleep. Her mind was filled with unfamiliar emotions she wanted to sort out. The concern Elliot had shown for her when he'd awakened from his fall down the stairs had moved her deeply. She watched the gentle rise and fall of his chest in the moonlight. She admired the sculpted lines that she had so carefully bathed earlier. What kind of a man was Elliot?

Stephanie's lips were pleasantly tender, and she could still taste the spicy warmth of Elliot's mouth. She raised a finger to her lips and touched them gently. They were warm and sensitive to her touch.

She had never been kissed like that before. Of course, she'd been kissed by other men, and it was usually pleasant enough. But not like this. Elliot's kiss had aroused feelings in her that she didn't recognize. His kiss had been a passionate union in itself. She wished he could have kissed her all night.

What would Elliot recall tomorrow? Probably nothing. When he'd kissed her, he had just been emerging from the fog of his fall. Maybe he hadn't even recognized her. Perhaps, in his disoriented state, he had kissed her thinking she was someone else. An unexpected stab of disappointment cut through her. No; he had spoken her name. He had looked into her eyes with recognition, she was certain of that.

Elliot murmured in his sleep and shifted an arm back behind his head. His open shirt fell back, exposing most of his chest to the moonlight. Stephanie felt the impulse to go to him, to caress the places she had felt under her searching fingers earlier. She longed to feel the spicy sweetness of his mouth on her mouth. Her cheeks grew hot with embarrassment at her own thoughts.

She shut her eyes. It certainly wouldn't do for Elliot to wake up and find her staring at him. She shook her head to shake the image of Elliot from her mind, but the more she tried to let it go, the more vivid it became. Of course, she had strong feelings toward him, the man had saved her life tonight! It was only natural that she might react this way.

She laid her head back against the chair. Everything will be alright in the morning she told herself sternly, although she knew it was a lie.

In a moment, she was asleep.

SEVEN

The dream began as it always did. The cheering in the locker room reverberated off the walls in a deafening chaos of echoes. He was surrounded by a solid mass of fellowship and good feelings. The air was thick with the smell of victory, of honest sweat and work and shared desire.

The cheering was for him. He'd played his best game ever today, and it was the big one, the national championship. His teammates pressed up against him, embracing him to them, absorbing and sharing in his glory. He was lifted up and carried around the room, the voices vibrating through his body, the power of the team lifting him so far up he'd never come down.

And tonight he would be with Siobhan. Beautiful, perfect Siobhan. She must be proud of him right now. God, how he loved her! Tonight he would make love to her until the sun came up again.

The locker room became the party, and the cheers and good times spilled on into the night, an endless dance of congratulations, toasts, and laughter. Siobhan was at his side now, her long hair falling back like a curtain of spun gold as she stretched up on her toes to kiss him. He put his hands around her small waist and lifted her up off her feet, holding her suspended until she shrieked with laughter and begged him to put her down. He glowed with pleasure to have her with him and he showed her off to all his friends with pride, hardly able to believe his good fortune to have her as his own.

The party noises faded away, and they were in bed at Siobhan's apartment, making love until the early light came, talking about the time after college and how their lives would be together.

He left her sleeping in the dawn, with a kiss on her nose and a note. He was still a little fuzzy from the night, but it was only a couple of blocks from Siobhan's apartment to his. His motorcycle started on the first kick, and the freshness of the morning blew through his hair. He inhaled deeply, filling his lungs with the cool promise of the new day.

The newspaper delivery van appeared out of nowhere, roaring around a corner, making up for lost time on its early morning route. He saw it for only a fraction of a second before it struck him broadside, shattering his right leg in a piercing white light of agony.

The hospital was all white, white everywhere, and he was on a cold table under a cold white light. The masked figures came and went, never speaking. He tried to talk to them, but nothing could come out of his mouth. He waited for Siobhan. She must be coming soon. Of course, she was. She loved him. He clung to the thought and tried to struggle through the mists that clouded his brain. Where was she?

And then Siobhan was there, reassuring and sympathetic. He searched her face for the comfort and love he had been waiting for, but found instead a strange coldness in her eyes. She looked at his injured leg with evaluating eyes that asked all the questions he hadn't let himself think about yet. She kissed him once, good-bye. He was alone in the white pain.

But the dream was different this time. As he faded in and out of his drugged consciousness, through the two surgeries and hours of therapy, he was not alone. No; this time someone was there with him, soothing him, ministering to his pain-racked body. Not Siobhan; someone else. Someone who carried a scent of lilacs with her. Someone whose hands were caring and gentle. Someone whose hair swept over his bare skin in a heavy auburn cloud.

Elliot woke up, stiff from his sleep on the too-short couch, but for a moment he remained still, staring at the ceiling. The images of his dream faded swiftly in the light of the dawn. He tried to hold onto them. The dream had been an unwelcome companion to his sleep for thirteen years, and he usually pushed it away as soon as he awoke, anxious to blot out the pain of the past with the concerns of the present. But this time, the dream ended not with the white pain, but with cool hands and lilacs.

Elliot sat up carefully. Every muscle of his body was sore, but everything seemed functional. He looked at the woman across from him.

Stephanie was asleep in the armchair, her long legs tucked up underneath her. A rush of tenderness came over him. She looked like a child who had stayed up past her bed time and had fallen asleep in the living room. Her head was resting against the right side of the chair and her face was serene. The muscles in his arms bunched tightly as he thought of the men who had tried to hurt her. If he'd been a few minutes later—

He didn't allow himself to complete the thought. She

needed to be protected, and to his great surprise he wanted to be the one to do it. Whatever might have happened between her and Martindale, she wasn't part of the embezzlement scam. She couldn't be. The two men last night had proven that. They had been looking for Stephanie. Well, let them try again. Next time he'd be ready.

He walked quietly in bare feet to the front door, dislodged the chair, and set it gently aside. He needed to get some air, to stretch his sore legs. More than that, the sight of her asleep like that was bringing back a haze of memories from the night. Had he really kissed her, or was that part of the dream? Either way, the remembrance of her mouth and her hands was driving him crazy. He shut the door quietly and headed out to the beach.

When Stephanie opened her eyes, Elliot was gone. The room was filled with a cold, steely light. She went to the window and looked out at the water. The ocean was flat and grey in the early morning light. She wasn't wearing her watch, but it couldn't be much past dawn.

Stephanie's neck was stiff from sleeping upright, and she felt fuzzy and disoriented. The events of last night came rushing back to her in a disorganized flood of images. The man grabbing her; the gunshot; Elliot's face disappearing backwards into the darkness. Elliot's mouth on hers; his hard chest beneath her fingers. She shook her head to try to clear the memories into some kind of order.

She opened the front door and a sharp pain stabbed through the back of her shoulder as she pulled it open. The light outside was brighter, and illuminated the landscape in an odd, flat way that gave the whole scene an unreal appearance. The ocean was like smooth pewter, an opaque, matte surface stretching out to the horizon.

Where was Elliot? She looked down the beach, but saw no one but a skinny brown dog trotting alongside the water toward some important canine destination.

She thought about Elliot's kiss last night. Involuntarily, she reached up to touch her lips. It was all circumstance, of course, said the logical part of her mind. Two people could hardly be less suited to one another. It was just the nature of their bizarre situation that had awakened these feelings in her.

And yet, the feelings were there. A desire, a fascination, a need to see him, to share with him. The memory of his concern and tenderness was overwhelming. Where was Elliot right now?

Stephanie went back inside and headed for the kitchen. She breezed quickly through the kitchen and unlocked the back door on the service porch. The red scooter was still by the clump of palms where Elliot had left it last night. She closed and locked the door and went back through the house out the front door.

Stephanie squinted down the beach. A figure was walking on the beach, coming toward the point. It was definitely a man, but she couldn't discern more than that. Her heart had a sudden flutter of fear. Who was it? Could it be one of the men from last night? She gripped the porch railing so tightly that her hands ached.

Relief flooded her body as she recognized him. It was Elliot. She saw the white trousers and bright shirt he had worn to dinner last night. She looked down at herself. The hem of her blue dress was filthy and torn. There was a spot of blood from where she'd scraped her knee on the rough floor of the wine cellar.

The wine cellar! She hadn't told Elliot about what

she'd found last night! She hiked up her dress and took off running down the beach toward Elliot. Her bare feet pounded on the damp sand. She felt a knot of excitement in her stomach. It seemed she had been away from him for a very long time.

"Elliot! Elliot, I never told you! I forgot to tell you last night!" She shouted to be heard over the ocean. Elliot looked surprised to see her running toward him in the early morning light. She stopped in front of him, out of breath, unable to speak. He looked at her quizzically as she caught her breath.

"Elliot! I almost forgot—I found it!"

"Found what? Are you alright?" His eyes were instantly alert and inquisitive. "What are you talking about?" Stephanie felt a sudden stab of embarrassment. Last night seemed months ago. She straightened the top of her dress, feeling uncomfortably exposed.

"Come with me." She turned and began to run back to the house. Elliot hesitated, then ran after her.

Back at the house, Stephanie sprinted up the stairs, Elliot close behind her. The wine cellar door was ajar.

Silently, Stephanie led Elliot inside and closed the door behind them. She flicked the light switch, and they squinted in the glare of the bare bulb. The computer hummed softly, waiting for them.

"What is this?" Elliot examined the equipment, clearly unfamiliar with its use.

"This is how they got to the money. By plugging a phone line into this modem," she tapped the small box next to the computer, "and calling up the mainframe computer at Martindale & Associates, this computer can function just like the computer in my office back in Newport!" Stephanie was breathless with excitement. "Do you follow?"

"No, I don't. Hold on a minute—do you mean to

tell me that anybody with a PC and a phone could break into your system and play havoc with it?"

"Of course not! Access to the computer is controlled by a multiple password security system that limits who can get into the computer and what functions they can use. Our employees have access only to what information they need to perform their own jobs, and what is appropriate for their level of responsibility." Stephanie crossed her arms over her chest. "The passwords are very closely guarded, and we change them every ten days."

"And where do the passwords come from?" Elliot's forehead was furrowed in concentration.

"The new passwords are random character strings—nonsense words, really—created by the computer. The new passwords are distributed to the heads of the various departments by the security administrator."

Elliot's eyes gleamed with understanding. "And the security administrator . . ."

"That's me."

"And Leo?"

"He had the highest level of access."

"So, who else had that level, besides you and Leo?"

"No one else did. Just me and Leo."

"So, the two of you were the only ones in your entire organization who had total control of the system?"

"That's right." Stephanie felt her back stiffen uncomfortably. What was Elliot getting at?

Elliot raised one eyebrow slightly. "It seems you and Leo shared just about everything."

Stephanie was filled with an icy anger.

"Elliot, I've tried to tell you the truth, but you don't want to listen!" Her voice was shaky, but she made herself continue. "There was nothing—is nothing—between Leo and me. He has been a good friend to me. That's all. You can believe whatever you like. I guess it really doesn't matter what you think.'' She turned and left him alone.

Stephanie took the stairs two at a time and was out the front door before Elliot reached the upper landing.

Alone on the beach, Stephanie was suddenly overwhelmed by a feeling of futility. She stopped walking. There was no point. She was in custody, and despite anything that happened last night, Elliot McKeon wasn't going to jeopardize his career over her. She was just a case to him, a way to realize his own goals. Any tenderness, any concern, any feelings between them were false.

The trip had been a failure. She had discovered the computer, but Elliot believed that only implicated her further! Why was it so important to her that Elliot believe in her innocence? She sat down on the sand in despair.

She saw Elliot watching her from the doorway of the house. Don't worry, she thought bitterly to herself, I'm not going anywhere. The morning sun had grown brighter, but she shivered in the damp sand. She was tired and dirty. Her shoulder throbbed with pain.

A small sailboat glided by on the smooth surface of the water. Leo liked to sail. Stephanie remembered how much he loved this place, but he always was glad to get back to work. He loved his business like some men loved their families.

Work was endlessly fascinating to him. Leo embraced new ideas in business with an unusual enthusiasm for a man of his age. It was Leo who had insisted that Martindale & Associates have the best, most up-to-date computer system in the industry, and instead of being satisfied with hiring the experts to implement it, he wanted to learn to use it himself as well.

He had built an empire from nothing, although he was, as he enjoyed reminding people, "Just a farm boy from Blythe." Could he have deliberately destroyed everything he had worked so hard to achieve? It was impossible for her to accept that answer.

Stephanie looked down at the sand and traced a pattern with her finger. She didn't realize Elliot was standing over her until he spoke.

"I'm sorry for not believing you about Leo. I can be pretty stubborn sometimes." Stephanie looked up. Elliot's eyes were gentle and apologetic. "For what it's worth, I believe you now."

"Well, if it had been true, I'd probably be with Leo now, wherever that is, and not sitting here on the beach wearing last night's dress." She smiled wanly.

Elliot's eyes swept over her. "I think you look great, especially considering what you've been through." He extended his hand to her. "Let's go back to the hotel."

Stephanie took his hand and let him pull her to her feet. "I guess there's no reason to stay here any longer."

Leo's house gleamed in the growing brightness. It was remarkably innocent looking in the morning. The white exterior looked freshly scrubbed, almost newly painted. It looked as though a happy family might emerge from its front door at any moment. If the house had any secrets about what had happened there, it wasn't giving them up.

They walked in silence back to the house. The sun had emerged now, and felt warm on Stephanie's bare back. They reached the front door. Stephanie stayed outside on the porch as Elliot went around to the side to get the scooter. She heard the small engine start, and he rode up to the front of the house.

"We're nearly out of gas. I think we can get some at that boat rental place back at the main road."

Stephanie climbed onto the back of the scooter, and Elliot headed back toward the road.

"Elliot, wait. I think I left my purse back at the house."

"What?" Elliot gunned the tiny engine.

"It's got everything in it, including my passport."

"Great." He drove the short distance back to the house. "You go in and find it. I'll see if I can get some gas and I'll be back to pick you up in a couple of minutes."

Stephanie hopped off the scooter. She headed into the house without a word and he rode away.

She'd had her purse with her when she left the restaurant last night. She must have dropped it somewhere in the house. Stephanie glanced quickly around the living room, then headed upstairs. In the wine cellar, she found her purse on the table next to the computer. The screen was still on from this morning. She reached for the switch on the side of the computer and turned it off. The machine's hum faded into silence.

Stephanie clutched her purse under her arm and headed for Leo's bedroom. The blood-stained sheets were a grim reminder of the seriousness of her situation. Her eyes swept over the now familiar contents of the room. She'd searched every corner of this house in such detail she felt she could almost take it apart and put it back together again in her sleep! There was no point in looking any further. If there were any clues to Leo's disappearance here, she would have found them by now.

She stepped out into the hall and closed the bedroom door behind her. She leaned wearily against it for a moment, and closed her eyes. Stephanie felt a nagging suspicion that she was forgetting something. What was that game they'd played as children? She couldn't remember the name, but it had something to do with hiding an object in plain sight of the person looking for it.

Bad example, she thought to herself. There's nothing here to find, in plain sight or otherwise. She opened her eyes and headed toward the stairs.

She passed the open door of the wine cellar. The dark, silent eye of the computer stared blankly out at her. Stephanie looked at it. What was it about this familiar object that was so ominous?

Realization exploded within her mind, banishing the fatigue that weighed her body down. She dropped her purse on the table and sat down in front of the dark screen. She flipped the switch and the screen blipped into life. She quickly signed on, then commanded the modem to dial the phone number of the data access line at Martindale & Associates. The computer answered on the fourth ring.

PLEASE ENTER USER IDENTIFICATION CODE:

S_ROBINSON, she typed in answer.

PLEASE ENTER PASSWORD:

VORPAL_SWORD

The computer paused as it processed Stephanie's input. In a moment, she was looking at the same screen that greeted her every morning when she arrived at her office in Newport.

She worked quickly, bypassing all the normal work-day functions, and entering the system maintenance mode of the computer. She needed the highest access code to enter this area of operation. An unauthorized person could effectively destroy the system from this point. Even the technical people who worked on the computer did not have the clearance to enter without direct approval from Stephanie or Leo.

Stephanie scrolled a directory of the files down the screen. There were thousands of them. She knew that there might be many more encrypted files that were invisible. Without knowing the file names, they were inaccessible to anyone but the person who had created them.

Like a needle in a haystack, Stephanie thought to herself grimly. *To find it, just move aside all the hay.* She went to work.

Elliot twisted the cap back on the tiny gas tank and wiped his hands on his once white trousers. He paid the sleepy attendant for the gas. The attendant grunted and went back to his task of refueling the tanks of the rental boats.

There were very few other vehicles on the road this early in such a remote area of the island. The morning was growing warmer, and the fragrance of the many different island flowers mingled with the salty smell of the air blowing in from the beach. Elliot inhaled the freshness of the morning and thought about Stephanie.

He hadn't been affected by a woman since Siobhan. He dated fairly frequently, mostly out of boredom, but rarely saw the same woman more than twice. The wives and girlfriends of his business associates were anxious to set him up, and he usually obliged. Sometimes he thought if he spent one more evening with an exquisitely groomed and coiffed beauty who thought habeas corpus was an Italian designer, the evening might end in bloodshed.

Stephanie was different. She was intelligent, ambitious, and opinionated. He found her challenging and irritating. Why had kissing her been so incredible?

His desire ran hot within him as he remembered her firm lips yielding to his kisses. He could still taste their spicy sweetness. He wanted her, more than he had wanted a woman for a long time. And soon, they would return to California, where he would do his best to put her in prison.

The porch was empty when he parked the scooter in front of the house. Was something wrong? Elliot took the front steps two at a time.

"Stephanie! Where are you?"

His heart was pounding with sudden panic. Why had he left her alone? He looked around the living room quickly and shoved open the door to the kitchen. No sign of her anywhere.

"Elliot! Elliot!" Stephanie's voice was coming from upstairs and was filled with an urgency that pierced Elliot's chest with fear. He nearly took the kitchen door off its hinges as he slammed through it back to the living room.

Stephanie was at the top of the stairs. Her hair was a wild mass around her face, and her eyes were flashing emerald fire.

"Elliot! I found it!"

_____ EIGHT _____

Elliot pounded up the stairs. He grabbed Stephanie firmly by the shoulders. His eyes searched her face for signs of distress.

"Are you alright?" His voice was rough with concern and relief.

"Elliot, I found it!" Stephanie's face was flushed and hot. "It was there all the time! I just didn't think about it!" Stephanie laughed happily, then kissed him suddenly, her lips firm and smooth against his. Relief, confusion, and desire warred within him as their lips crushed together.

The woman has completely flipped, Elliot thought. He held tightly to her arms, reassuring himself that she was safe.

"Stephanie, what are you talking about?" He tried to keep his voice gentle, but she wasn't making sense. Maybe the stress had finally gotten to her.

"The computer! Leo left a message! It's not much, but he was probably being watched closely. Come on!" She broke loose from his grasp and hurried down the hall to the wine cellar. Elliot followed close behind.

Stephanie sat in front of the computer's screen. "Watch," she commanded. Her fingers flew on the keys. Elliot watched her suspiciously. What was going on?

The keys clicked under her fingers. Stephanie studied the screen intently. "Look at this."

The screen filled with rows of glowing characters.

»DIRECTORY OF DRIVE M:\ IS NONCOM.BAT

»DIR LISTING:

»MASTERDIR.COM	»FILEDIR.COM	»LISTDIR.COM
»SLIPDISK1.COM	»SLIPDISK2.COM	»SLIPDISDK3.COM
»SLIPBAT.BAT	»FILESIZE.BAT	»FILESIZE.TXT
»AUTOEXEC.BAT	»AUTOEXEC.TXT.	»MASTERDIR.BAT

The list scrolled on until the screen was filled, over and over again. When it finally stopped, it read

»6897 FILES IN DRIVE M:\ NONCOM.BAT

»17 HIDDEN FILES

Stephanie's eyes glowed with excitement and hope. "Do you see?" She gestured triumphantly toward the screen.

Elliot was baffled. "No, I don't." *What was she talking about? Had she lost her mind?*

"The hidden files, Elliot! They contain the operating system itself, the programs that drive the computer. There should only be sixteen! When I saw there was a new one, I knew Leo had created it. I just needed to find it."

Her fingers flashed over the computer's key board. "I tried all the file names I could think of—all the passwords, code words, everything. His name, my name, his birthday, crazy things." She pushed back a strand of hair off her face. "But I didn't find anything." She demonstrated.

```
>>TYPE STEPHANIE.HID
>>NO FILE FOUND
>>TYPE ROBINSON.HID
>>NO FILE FOUND
>>TYPE LEO.HID
>>NO FILE FOUND
```

"Then I got lucky. Watch this."

```
>>TYPE SMOKEY.HID
***
17–53–52/87–58–48
***
```

Stephanie leaned back in her chair. "There it is." She turned to Elliot. He was very confused.

"What the hell is—" He broke off and regarded Stephanie with suspicion. "Who's Smokey?"

"Leo's dog! Black Lab, he's had him for years. He treats him like a child, absolutely spoiled rotten. I've even had to baby-sit a few times myself." She seized his right hand and held it captive between her two smaller ones. "Don't you see, Elliot! Leo left this for me! He knew I'd be left behind in this mess. He probably only had a few seconds to create this file to give us a clue about what's happened!"

The adrenaline pumping through Elliot's body took another jump. His excitement went beyond Stephanie's discovery. His heart was pounding because of the woman who was squeezing his hand with all her strength, and whose deep green eyes shimmered with hope.

Stephanie was innocent. She could be trusted. The revelation filled him with a rush of elation. He felt like shouting the news to the world, but instead he kissed her once, quickly, then stood. His eyes narrowed down to two bright blue slits.

"Account number. Bank account here in the Caymans, or maybe even Switzerland." He started to pace in the tiny room. "We can get started this morning. We should start with the largest bank here. If it's not one of their account numbers, maybe they can identify which bank it belongs to."

Stephanie carefully copied down the information on the screen. Her excitement was eroding as she realized the enormity of their task. There were thousands of banks here! She knew that they would not receive much cooperation from the officials. If only Leo had left a more specific message for them!

"Let's get going." Elliot waited impatiently at the door of the tiny room. "We'd better stop by the hotel first and make ourselves respectable."

Stephanie watched Elliot carefully close the hidden door behind them. He reached into the dark space behind the hidden panel to secure the door. She could see the outline of the hard muscles of his back through his shirt. She wanted to touch him, to feel him again. What did he remember of last night?

Satisfied that the false door was firmly back in place, Elliot turned back to Stephanie. Had he felt her eyes on him? He put his arms around her waist and drew her to him. Wordlessly, he kissed her, slowly this time. She put her arms around him and returned the kiss. His overnight growth of beard scratched gently against her face.

He pulled her firmly to him, and she felt the strength of his body against her breasts. She gave herself up to his probing tongue. His mouth demanded her fully, consumed her completely. She closed her eyes, and reality faded away.

For this moment, nothing existed except the two of them, their bodies tightly pressed to one another. She felt his muscles move beneath his clothes. His hands caressed the bare skin of her shoulders and back. Her hands explored him in return, only the thin fabric of his shirt between her probing fingers and his body. Stephanie felt a stab of desire for him that was almost painful. She realized she wanted to make love to him.

Stephanie opened her eyes. The spell of unreality was broken. They were standing in the hall of a deserted house on a grey morning wearing the same clothes they'd been wearing since yesterday. She had a job to do. They needed to get started. She pulled away from Elliot's hungry mouth.

"Elliot, we need to get going." His eyes were searching her face, but she wasn't sure what he was looking for. He took his hands from her waist.

"Okay." He smiled a little crookedly. "The carriage awaits." Stephanie followed him down the stairs.

They rode back to town in silence. Stephanie held on to the strap of the seat and was nearly bounced off several times.

"You'd be more secure if you held on to me," said Elliot. Stephanie said nothing, but continued to hold onto the strap. Touching Elliot was too risky.

When they reached the hotel, Stephanie saw the same man was on duty behind the desk who had been there when they left for dinner the night before. She could see his imagination going crazy, but she walked by the desk with as much dignity as she could manage. The man openly stared at them, but said nothing.

Stephanie fumbled in her purse for the key to her room. Elliot leaned against the wall next to the door. Stephanie unlocked the door, then turned back to Elliot. His translucent blue eyes swept over her, drinking her in as a man might a breathtaking view. She was suddenly aware of her ragged appearance.

"Well, I've got to take a shower. We've got a lot of work to do."

"Yes." His face, darkened slightly by a day's growth of whiskers, was thoughtful.

"I know I haven't said it yet." Stephanie touched his arm gently. "Thank you for last night. You saved my life."

Elliot gave an exaggerated shrug. "Aw shucks, ma'am. 'Tweren't nothin'." He smiled, the light glinting off the small chip in his tooth. "I'll be back for you in forty-five minutes." He headed down the hall, then turned back.

"Be careful." His voice was serious.

"Don't worry, I will." She started to close the door.

"Stephanie."

"Yes?" She leaned back out into the hall. Elliot had taken a step back toward her door.

"Lock your door."

Stephanie nodded silently and closed the door with a firm click.

Inside his room, Elliot started the water running in the shower. He stripped off his clothes and dropped them in a pile on the floor. He examined his naked body in the mirror. He'd picked up some pretty nasty looking bruises in his fall down the stairs last night. His ribs hurt like hell. He checked the cut on his scalp. It looked like it was healing quickly. The ragged slash on his calf was doing okay. Stephanie had done a good job of cleaning him up and tending to his injuries.

As he thought of her, and her hands on his body, he was hit with an embarrassing hot wave of desire. Damn it, why did she have that effect on him? Of course, she was attractive; in fact, she was probably the sexiest woman he'd ever met, but that wasn't what this was about. Even in that filthy dress this morning, her hair matted and eyes bleary from lack of sleep, he had felt something for her that was not familiar to him. Desire, yes; but mingled with a fascination that he'd never felt for a woman before.

He wanted to make love to Stephanie Robinson; there was no denying that. But he already knew that the simple physical act alone would not satisfy the strength of his need. His desire demanded a greater intimacy than they might find in bed together. He wanted to find out what she thought about things, discover how her mind worked, learn about her feelings. He needed to know her, to know everything about her. He'd thought he would never feel that for a woman again. But most of all, he wanted to finally trust someone completely again after so many years of caution, and that scared the hell out of him.

Elliot stepped into the shower and adjusted the taps, making the water cooler and cooler. In a few seconds, the water was icy cold. He turned his bruised body beneath the sharp needles of water, rinsing the dirt and sweat from him. He closed his eyes and turned his face directly into the stinging stream and tried to put Stephanie Robinson out of his mind.

* * *

Stephanie stepped out of the shower and quickly toweled off. She found a pair of khaki slacks and a short sleeve white cotton blouse in her luggage. With some flat walking shoes, it was a plain but comfortable outfit.

She used a second towel to dry her hair as thoroughly as she could, and combed out the tangles carefully. She briefly considered makeup when she saw the dark circles under her eyes, but decided against it. She had a job to do. This was no time for vanity. Who was she fixing herself up for anyway? Elliot?

Stephanie thought about kissing Elliot on the landing this morning. Her fingers tingled with the memory of his body. She could almost taste his kisses. The memory brought a warm flush that she felt over her whole body. What was wrong with her?

She sat down on the bed and silently gave herself a stern lecture. Stephanie told herself that what had happened last night and again this morning on the stairs, was understandable, after what they'd been through together. It was natural, probably even healthy, to feel an attraction to someone who had saved your life. But that's what it was, a natural reaction to a very strange, unfamiliar sequence of events.

But natural or not, she couldn't stop it with her logical reasoning. Stephanie was used to being in control, and this feeling was the most out-of-control sensation she'd ever encountered before. That frightened her.

She lay back on the bed. So many things had happened. She needed to take care of herself now. As desperately as she wanted to, it was a mistake to look to Elliot, or anyone else, to take care of her. She was on her own. She had to remember that.

She closed her eyes and tried to think about Leo and the missing money. What were the chances of finding the account that belonged to the numbers hidden in the computer? Why hadn't Leo given her more to go on? He had probably endangered himself to even leave the information he did. He had done his best. Now it was up to her.

She sat up restlessly. Where was Elliot? He'd been gone an hour! Stephanie opened the door and looked down the hall. No sign of him. It was almost 11:00 a.m. Had he said they were to meet in the lobby? She couldn't remember. Maybe he was pacing the lobby right now, checking his watch. She grabbed her purse and room key and closed the door behind her.

Elliot wasn't waiting in the tiny lobby. Stephanie considered asking the man behind the desk if he'd seen him, but decided against it. She stepped out into the bright sunlight.

The hotel was on a small, one-way street that led out onto a larger street leading to the bay. Stephanie walked the three short blocks to the corner and looked toward the water. There was no sign of Elliot anywhere. She stepped into the small grocery store on the corner and looked around.

A tired looking woman stood at the cash register, nursing a steaming cup of coffee. She nodded wearily to Stephanie between sips. Stephanie smiled and quickly looked up and down the few aisles of groceries. No Elliot. She nodded to the woman and stepped back outside just in time to see a figure burst from the hotel lobby out onto the street.

Elliot rapped firmly on the hotel room's thin door. He waited a moment, then knocked again more loudly. Cold needles of worry began to prick at the back of his neck. Why wasn't she answering? He knocked again, this time so hard the flimsy door shook under his knuckles. He put his ear against the door. Silence. Hesitating only a moment, he laid his left shoulder against the door and shoved hard. The cheap latch gave way under the powerful thrust and the door opened inward, slamming against the wall.

The room was empty. Stephanie's shoulder bag was undisturbed on the bed. Her purse was gone from the dresser. Elliot crossed the room in two steps and shoved the bathroom door open. The mirror was fogged with steam, and damp towels were hung neatly on the hook on the back of the door. He stepped back into the room and surveyed it one more time. In spite of the normal appearance of the room, Elliot's concern intensified. After what had almost happened last night, how could he have left her alone and unprotected? Where was she? He pushed back the dark images of menace that flooded into his mind. He had to find Stephanie. He slammed the door behind him, and the echo reverberated down the hall as he ran toward the lobby.

Stephanie waved to the figure in front of the hotel. Elliot was pacing madly back and forth in front of the doors. He was wearing worn jeans and a white cotton shirt. Relieved, she hurried to meet him, running the last two blocks. Elliot met her halfway, his long legs carrying him purposefully toward her.

"Where in the hell have you been?" He grabbed her roughly by the arm. "You weren't in your room!" His eyes blazed with a dangerous fire.

"You were late. I was anxious to get started. I thought maybe you'd gone in the grocery store for something—Let go of my arm." Stephanie's voice was contained. She was surprised at how angry he was. She'd seen his temper before, but its volatility still disturbed her.

"What do you mean by running off like that! When

I tell you to wait for me, I mean wait!'' He released her arm, and turned away suddenly. ''Let's go.'' He headed down the street toward the water, walking quickly.

Stephanie stood still in stunned surprise. Elliot McKeon was the most irritating, unpredictable man she'd ever met! She stood fuming as his back disappeared around the corner. Well, she was sick and tired of being treated like she was a disobedient child, and she was going to tell him so!

She broke into a run to catch up with him. When she reached the corner, she looked up and down the busy street, squinting into the bright morning sun.

Elliot was nowhere in sight.

NINE

"No. Absolutely not."

The thin man behind the desk shook his head, and the glare of the fluorescent lights overhead turned the round lenses of his glasses into blank circles. Stephanie saw her face reflected back to her in them.

"Mr. Stickly, I know you must protect your customers' privacy, but I assure you that this is a matter of great concern to the authorities in the United States." Stephanie was using her best we're-all-professionals-here manner, but the man was not budging. "I wouldn't ask that any account be identified without proper authorization. If you could just confirm this as one of your account numbers—"

"Miss Robinson." Stickly leaned forward and dropped his already hushed voice even lower. "A discussion of this nature—however theoretical—is an intolerable violation of the secrecy our customers are guaranteed by this institution." He plastered an oily strand of his thinning hair back in its place on his pink scalp. "I should not have let this conversation continue as far as

117

it already has.'' His forehead glistened with nervous sweat. He stood up to dismiss her.

"I'm sorry, but I am unable to discuss this matter any further, Miss Robinson.''

Stickly escorted her to the large glass front doors. He opened the door for her, looking nervously back at the other employees at work. When she was on the other side, he stood wedged in the partly-open doorway, his face betraying the agony of his indecision. He checked over his shoulder, then spoke quickly. "It's not one of our numbers.'' He stepped back inside and walked back to the desk with frightened, mincing little steps.

Stephanie felt a wave of despair. It was already three, and she'd only managed to visit three banks. The first two had been even less cooperative. She wondered if Elliot was having any more success than she was. There were hundreds of banks on the island!

The business district of George Town had been humming with activity this morning, but now things had quieted down to the pace of a lazy tropical afternoon. The bank faced a quaint plaza, bordered with shops offering fine jewelry, silks, perfumes, china, and elaborately carved pieces of rare black coral. Stephanie sat down wearily on a bench.

The afternoon sun was warm, and she could smell the ocean a few blocks away. She closed here eyes. Where was Elliot? She felt a surge of anger at the memory of their scene in front of the hotel. Elliot was so damn unpredictable! Of course, she was angry at the way he'd treated her; anyone would be. But it hurt her far more to be treated like that by someone who had shown such care and consideration to her; a man who had risked his life for hers.

Stephanie let her anger ebb away. She missed Elliot.

Somehow, her fate had seemed much brighter when they were together. It was as simple as that. Now she was alone, and everything seemed hopeless again.

Stephanie opened her eyes and considered her options. Now that it was after 3:00, banking hours were over. She was convinced that she wouldn't get much further at any of the other banks. Besides, the chances of her wandering into the right bank, and talking to anyone there who might remember Leo were ridiculously slim.

A young policeman walked by, resplendent in his uniform. He gave Stephanie a winning smile and tipped his cap politely to her as he passed. She smiled back wanly, thinking *if only you could help me*. She knew that it would be pointless to seek the local police's help in the matter of the missing money. At this point, they would regard it as a purely civil matter. If one of their banks had received a large deposit, what of it? As far as they would be concerned, no crime had been committed in the Caymans.

She took off her sunglasses and rubbed her eyes. She might as well keep walking. She put her sunglasses back on and headed toward the ocean.

The Caribbean sparkled azure in the afternoon sunlight. A variety of boats were moored in the harbor: big, flat barges that accommodated large groups of scuba divers out to the famous coral reefs and caverns; glass-bottomed boats for the less adventurous to see the underwater world; and in the outer area of the harbor, a large, white cruise ship.

Stephanie crossed the street to walk along the edge of the harbor. The harbor was bordered by small gift shops selling cheap souvenirs and T-shirts. A block ahead, she saw a dive shop with a dock. On the other side of the building was a primitive mural of a scuba diver underwater, surrounded by sea turtles and an array of fanciful looking fish in bright colors. There was even a sea serpent and a mermaid. Above the mural in peeling letters was "CAPTAIN DON'S UNDERWATER ADVENTURES."

One of the dive boats was loading in preparation for departure. She stood at the railing at the top of the stairs leading down to the dock and watched the divers load their gear. Two young men were supervising the operation.

One of the two, a muscular blond kid who looked about nineteen or twenty, was staring at her from his station on the dock below. He said something to the other dive master and came up the steps to the railing where she was standing.

"We're diving Eden Rock. I've got an empty space on the boat. Want to come along?" His smile was a dazzling expanse of white teeth in a darkly tanned face.

"Thanks, but I don't dive." She smiled in apology.

"You can keep me company, then. I'm staying topside today with the boat. Jerry's the one getting wet this dive." He jerked a thumb over his shoulder at the other dive master, a skinny kid with bad skin, who was helping the last few divers find a spot to gear up on the boat. "My name's Billy."

"I'm Stephanie." He reminded her of the kid that worked as a messenger part-time for Martindale & Associates. What was his name? That seemed a thousand years ago.

"Well, how about it? Eden Rock isn't far, just in the outer harbor as a matter-of-fact, and it's a nice boat ride this time of day. It sure beats standing here in the heat letting the cars blow dust on you. Besides," he looked around with elaborate caution. "I won't charge you since you won't be diving. Come on! What do you say?"

Suddenly, Stephanie's attention was caught by two figures on another dock about thirty yards away. They appeared to be watching the dive boat. Even at this distance, Stephanie recognized them immediately. They were the men who had attacked her last night. Instantly, fear solidified into a heavy mass in her stomach.

Could they see her? Had they followed her here? Maybe they had been following her all day, waiting for the right opportunity to finish what they had started last night! She shivered in spite of the afternoon sun. She had been alone all afternoon! Where was Elliot?

Billy's voice startled her. "We'll only be out two hours. I'll have you back in time for a drink at sunset."

Stephanie made her decision. The two men were now at the street level, several blocks away. They were moving quickly.

"Great. Let's go." Stephanie hoped her fear wasn't obvious. Billy escorted her down the steps to the dock. He jumped lightly on board the boat and turned back to give Stephanie a hand. They picked their way through the divers getting their equipment ready, to the ladder that led to the upper level, and the small wheel house.

Billy started the engine. Jerry cast off the lines and jumped back on the boat as it pulled smoothly away from the dock. Stephanie stood in the doorway of the wheelhouse, as Billy eased the boat back from the dock out into the deeper waters of the large harbor.

Up on the street level, the two men were leaning against the railing watching the boat head out.

Stephanie stepped into the tiny wheelhouse. There was barely room, but she wanted to get out of sight. Billy looked at her with surprise.

"I don't know anything about boats," Stephanie said in flustered explanation. "Maybe you could show me how this thing works." The dock was far away now, and the people walking along the street were tiny figures in the distance. She couldn't see if the men were still there, but somehow she could feel their eyes watching the boat. They would be waiting for her when the boat returned after the dive.

"Running a cattle boat like this one isn't hard." Billy gave Stephanie his dazzling toothy smile, unaware of the fear pounding through her veins like ice water. "This is the wheel, just like a car. There are the throttles for the engines."

Stephanie nodded with a feigned enthusiasm. The dock was no longer discernable from the rest of the shore line.

"Billy, let's anchor this monster. We've still got to do the pre-dive briefing." Jerry stuck his head in the door of the wheelhouse. When he saw Stephanie, he glared at Billy. "You know you're not supposed to allow passengers in there!"

"You just take care of the anchor. We'll do the pre-dive in five minutes." Jerry disappeared, grumbling to himself.

"I'm sorry, I didn't want to get you in any trouble."

"Don't worry about it. Jerry's a real stickler about the rules." Billy chuckled and shifted the boat into reverse.

"What are you doing?"

"We want to be right over the reef. That way, the divers should be able to drop right down onto the dive site without too much swimming. They can conserve their air and spend more time on the site." He shifted into neutral. When he felt the anchor catch, he shut down the engines.

"Time to talk diving." Billy climbed down the ladder to the lower deck, where the divers were assembling their gear.

Stephanie wandered restlessly around the deserted upper deck. Below her, she could hear Billy wrap up the briefing and start to assist divers into the water. Soon the water was dotted with divers on the surface, who adjusted their gear and disappeared into the blue water below, leaving trails of bubbles behind.

Stephanie's mind was racing. Billy had said the dive would last about forty-five minutes. After getting everyone back in the boat and returning to shore, it would be close to sunset. What should she do if the men were there when the boat docked? She had to form a plan. If they weren't there, should she try to make it to the hotel? Even if she ran, it would be dark before she got there. Maybe she would be safer on the streets, or in some public place like a bar or restaurant.

She had to find Elliot. Elliot would know what to do. He would take care of her. He would— Don't be a fool, she lectured herself bitterly. You need Elliot, just like he needs you. What you and Elliot have is an arrangement, a business arrangement. Nothing more.

Stephanie sat down wearily on the bench behind the wheelhouse. She leaned back against the warm wood. A colorful map of the Caribbean was stapled up on the outside wall of the wheelhouse, underneath a layer of plastic. She stared at it without really seeing it.

Stephanie heard the divers coming aboard below her. She went to the map and found the three splashes of color that were the Caymans. She traced their outlines with her finger. Such a tiny area to search. Why did she feel so hopeless? She let her fingers wander over the map, finding the other islands, some of the names she recognized, some she'd never heard of: Jamaica, Cuba, Martinique, Barbados, St. Lucia, Turks and Caicos, Mayaguana. Little, irregular blotches scattered haphazardly through the precise quadrants formed by the latitudinal and longitudinal lines. Man's attempt to give order to a disorderly world.

The engines started, drowning out the excited chatter of the divers below. She looked around for Billy, but he was navigating from the other wheel on the lower level. He was deep in conversation with a blond girl in a peach bikini who was toweling herself dry.

Stephanie felt the boat begin to move. Her stomach was queasy, but it wasn't from the motion of the boat. She sat back down on the bench. The colors of the map seemed to run and blend together in the light of the sunset. It would be nearly dark by the time they arrived.

Elliot slammed the telephone down with a force that threatened to crack the receiver. He stepped out of the phone booth and squinted into the sunset. Where the hell was she? He'd checked the hotel for messages five times, and the last time the clerk had recognized his voice, said "No messages!" and hung up before he'd even asked.

Elliot felt like he'd been over every inch of George Town on foot today. He'd finally hired a cab to drive him street by street through the town, but after an hour he gave up on that method, paid the huge fare, and went back to searching on foot. Now it would be night soon, and he'd found no trace of Stephanie.

He'd been a fool to lose his temper this morning. His fear for her safety had vented itself in anger when he'd found her safe in front of the hotel. The thought of harm coming to her had shaken him up far more than he would admit, and anger had been a natural cover. Ever since they'd become separated he'd been berating himself for his stupidity, his arrogance, his carelessness. He tortured himself with memories of what had happened at Martindale's house last night; of what might be happening right now.

Had he been wrong about her? Maybe he had been set up. Maybe he had played his part in her plan, and now she was with Martindale, drinking a toast to his stupidity.

No. He had been right, his instinct and his brain told him that. Stephanie was innocent. He remembered the sound of her muffled cry on the landing; the two men touching her; the sound of the shot ripping the night in two. He remembered waking up to her caring for his injured body.

The only woman who had moved him in thirteen years was somewhere alone in this town, and he wasn't the only one who was trying to find her. Others were looking for her as well. He wiped the sweat off his forehead with the back of one hand and ran down the street toward the harbor.

TEN

The hand was over Stephanie's mouth before the slightest sound escaped. Another arm encircled her waist roughly, and pulled her from the twilight of the dock through a doorway into musty, thick blackness. There was a loud mechanical roaring, very close, and a smell of oil. The door was kicked closed behind her.

She saw nothing but the blackness. Sinewy arms held her pinned back against the hard male torso. She struggled, but there was no slack in her assailant's grip. Some buried primal instinct told her she would never free herself by strength, but still she fought with the wild abandon of a trapped she-wolf.

She jerked her head back sharply, managing to free her mouth enough to sink her teeth into the flesh of the man's hand with savage force. The man shuddered from the pain, but did not release her. He pulled her head back, and she felt his breath at her ear.

"Stephanie, it's me."

Elliot! Relief, confusion, and anger flooded her in successive waves. He didn't release her, or remove his

126

hand from her mouth. Where were they? What was going on?

"Don't make a sound." Elliot's tone left no room for argument. He slowly took his hand away from her mouth, and turned her around to face him. He pulled her to him and kissed her, tightly, intensely, possessively. He crushed her to his chest.

Elliot released her, and taking both her hands, led her deeper into the darkness, toward the source of the deafening noise. Elliot moved with confidence, carefully guiding them around unseen obstacles.

Stephanie's eyes were gradually adjusting to the darkness. They were now at the back wall of the room, and she could make out a large piece of equipment. Metal cylinders were stacked up on the opposite wall. Scuba tanks. The machine must be the air compressor used to fill the tanks.

The compressor was set out about four feet from the wall. Elliot motioned her into the narrow space behind the roaring machine. She hesitated a moment, then slid along hugging the wall with her back, with Elliot close behind.

The noise was deafening, and the hot, oily smell of machinery laboring made the air seem too thick to breathe. Stephanie looked to Elliot, her eyes filled with unspoken questions. Elliot then put his mouth close to her ear.

"They were waiting for you." Stephanie understood instantly. Rivulets of sweat were forming under her arms. She pulled Elliot's ear to her lips.

"Are they still out there?" She knew the answer without asking, yet was compelled to seek confirmation of her fear.

Elliot nodded without speaking.

She had thought she was safe. She had waited until

all the other passengers had unloaded their gear and boarded the shuttle bus to take them back to their hotels. Once the bus left, the dock and the dive shop appeared deserted.

The blond girl who had been talking to Billy on the trip back lingered behind, flirting with him as he finished his work. Billy didn't notice when Stephanie finally left the boat.

The compressor coughed twice, then shut down with a wheeze. The silence that followed seemed louder to Stephanie than the noise had been.

Stephanie could make out Elliot's face in the darkness now. His jaw was set, and she could see the pulsing of a vein in his neck echoing the strong, steady beat of his heart.

Elliot's body tensed further, in response to something she couldn't yet hear. Then suddenly, Stephanie heard it, too. Footsteps. They were not alone.

"Close that door behind you, Ben. We don't want no surprises." A razor-cold chill ripped up Stephanie's spine. It was the same Cockney twang she remembered from last night at Leo's house. In her mind's eye she clearly saw his face, his dirty red hair and filthy beard.

"Find the damn lights, Ben! I can't see a damn thing."

Ben grunted. There was a scraping sound like one of them had tripped over something.

"Hold on a minute, it's here somewheres—"

Stephanie heard voices outside, coming from the direction of the water. She recognized Billy's booming laugh. A moment later, two sets of footsteps were coming from the boat, heading toward the compressor room. Stephanie heard the Cockney shush Ben. The door swung open and banged against the wall inside.

"Let me just stack these tanks inside. I can wait until

tomorrow to fill them.'' Billy's voice was followed by the hollow metallic ring of the tanks banging together. Stephanie stopped breathing. Elliot was like stone beside her. She could almost reach out with her mind and feel the two men, standing as silently as she and Elliot were, holding their breath in the darkness.

"Billy! Billy, where the hell are you?'' The thick voice bellowed from upstairs. "I pay you to work, not womanize!'' The voice was swallowed up by a dry, hacking cough. "Get up here right now, or—'' More coughing and snorting sounds were followed by the sound of a window slamming.

"Damn it! It's Captain Don! I'll have to go calm him down.'' The last tank clanked loudly. "Wait for me in my jeep out front, okay? I won't be long.'' The blond murmured something too low to hear, then giggled. The door slammed shut. Footsteps faded toward the street.

There was an audible exhalation of relief from Ben and the Cockney. Stephanie and Elliot were silent, but Stephanie could hear the beating of her pulse in her ears.

The compressor jumped into life with a steady, throbbing beat that hadn't been there before. Stephanie let her breath go, and filled her grateful lungs with a new gulp of the thick, stale air. She became aware that she was gripping Elliot's arm so tightly that the flow of blood to her fingers had been stopped. She loosened her grip slightly, and needles of pain pierced her hand.

The darkness flickered slightly. Had the door been opened and shut again? Stephanie thought she heard it, but the compressor made it impossible to be sure. Elliot motioned her to stay, and slipped out from behind the compressor, disappearing into the darkness of the room.

Stephanie's head was swimming. Sweat was dripping

into her eyes, and she wiped it away with the back of her hand. Her lungs were burning from the tainted air. Her eyes ached from straining to see in the blackness. She shut them tightly against the hot metallic air.

She jumped with fright as a hand closed strongly on her wrist. Elliot drew her out of the small cramped space. He held her to him for a moment. They were alone.

He released her, and motioned toward the door. Stephanie took a step, and felt her legs give way beneath her. Her knees hit the rough wooden floor with painful force. She stopped her fall with a palm flat on the floor. Her stomach surged, and she was afraid she might vomit.

Elliot's arms were around her. She felt him pull her up to her feet with a sense of urgency. He opened the door into the night. The fresh ocean air rushed over them like a wave. Elliot swept her up and half carried, half dragged her up the stairs to the street. She took long, deep breaths, but still felt as if she were suffocating.

"Put your arm around my neck." Elliot put her left arm around his neck, locking it there with his left hand, and put his right arm around her waist, lifting most of her weight off her feet. "Now walk. Walk!"

Elliot's voice seemed to come from a great distance, even though he was right beside her. Stephanie forced herself to listen and obey. She concentrated on putting one foot in front of the other. She let no other thoughts enter her mind. Walk. Walk. One step at a time. She closed her eyes. Walk. Walk. Walk.

Stephanie awoke to the sound of water. The rushing, trickling sound seeped through the layers of sleep, reaching her dreams. Her mind was thick, reluctant to awake. She moved, and felt the soreness of her muscles. The pain helped bring her to consciousness.

She was in her hotel room. The room was filled with the grey light of very early morning. She looked around the room and recognized her clothes from yesterday laid out neatly on the wicker chair by the window. She realized that she was completely naked between the smooth cool sheets.

The water stopped, and in its absence, Stephanie immediately recognized what it had been. Someone had just finished showering in her bathroom.

ELEVEN

Stephanie drew the sheet up tightly under her chin. She looked around the hotel room in confusion. A man's shaving kit was sitting open on the dresser.

She quickly ran through the events of last night in her mind, recalling everything with terrifying clarity. But sometime after she and Elliot had escaped from the compressor room, it was as if a light switch had been turned off in her brain. She remembered nothing that had happened after that point.

Elliot appeared in the doorway to the bathroom, wearing only a white towel wrapped low around his waist. He was drying his hair with another towel, rubbing his head vigorously. He stopped when he saw that Stephanie was awake, freezing in mid-rub, his uplifted arms accentuating the massive wedge of his upper body.

"Hi. I hope I didn't wake you." His smile was warm and reassuring, but Stephanie didn't feel reassured. Elliot gave his hair one last swipe, then hung the towel on the hook on the back of the bedroom door. He went to the dresser and dug through the leather shaving kit. He found a comb, and looking at himself in the mirror over the dresser, proceeded to comb his tangled hair. Stephanie stared silently at the muscles moving in his broad, naked back. The damp towel fit snugly, revealing the hard muscles of his buttocks moving as he shifted his weight slightly.

Satisfied with his hair, Elliot turned back toward the bed. Stephanie pulled the sheet up even more tightly, so only her head was visible. She searched for words, but found none.

Elliot leaned back against the dresser and looked at her, resting his elbows behind him. A slight sheen of moisture from the shower still covered his torso. Little droplets of water glistened in the dark hair covering the breadth of his chest. His dark nipples were tight from the change in temperature. Stephanie realized with a rush of embarrassment that she was staring at him. She drew her knees more tightly together.

"How are you feeling today?" He spoke casually, as if he were quite used to talking to her while she was naked in bed, and he himself almost as exposed. "I was pretty worried about you last night."

"What are you doing here? I mean, what happened?" Stephanie felt foolish, like a drunk waiting to hear about last night's forgotten escapades from a more sober companion. "I mean, I remember being in that little room, and the men, and Billy, but how did I . . ." She looked around the room. "I mean, how did we . . ."

"You passed out on me cold. I pretty much carried you back to the hotel. Must have been the fumes from the compressor, plus I guess I probably gave you a good scare when I grabbed you that way." He crossed his arms across his naked chest. "I didn't want to be rough, but I needed to get you out of the way fast. Those two—"

Stephanie cut him off. "I know. Thanks for being

there. Again.'' She shifted under the covers. ''Excuse me for being dense, but I seem to be, ah, naked under here, and you . . .'' She gestured in Elliot's general direction.

Elliot looked down at his towel. ''Oh. Sorry.'' He picked up a pair of jeans from the floor and slipped them on, discretely keeping the towel secured around his waist until they were on. Stephanie watched his scarred knee disappear into the denim. He dropped the towel and buttoned the waistband. The jeans rode low on his lean hips.

''After I got you back to the hotel, you were pretty dirty, not to mention soaked with sweat. I was afraid you'd get chilled, so I undressed you, toweled you down good and put you to bed.''

''You undressed . . .'' Stephanie felt herself blushing a deep shade of scarlet. The hot flush spread from her face down her neck to her chest, continuing down her body in a warm wave to her toes.

''Look, its not like I've never seen a naked woman before,'' he said brusquely. ''Besides, I think you might have been in a mild state of shock. I wasn't about to leave you alone, so I slept here with you.'' Elliot smiled wryly at the expression on Stephanie's face. ''Don't worry, your virtue's still intact. I slept on the floor.''

''Do you mind, I need to . . .'' Stephanie gestured toward the bathroom.

''No problem.'' Elliot zipped up his shaving kit. ''I'm going back to my room to get dressed. I want you to lock this door behind me and put a chain on it.''

He crossed to the door and put his hand on the knob. ''I'll be back to pick you up in twenty minutes.'' His eyes were suddenly steely. ''Whatever you do, don't open the door for anyone until I get back. Do you understand?''

Stephanie nodded mutely. Elliot started to open the door, but turned back. There was a flood of high color in his face. His gaze was like a palpable touch that lingered over her body, warming where it touched.

"Let's get one thing straight. If I were going to make love to you, it wouldn't be like that, with you practically passed out and me taking advantage of a bad situation." His eyes flicked coolly over her shoulders, bare where the sheet had pulled down. She saw the memory of her naked body reflected in his eyes. The thought gave her a strange jittery feeling just beneath her breastbone.

His cobalt eyes locked hers and held them for a moment in silent challenge. When he spoke again his voice had a dark, rough edge to it that vibrated deep within her. "You'd be awake, and you'd stay awake. I guarantee it."

He shut the door behind him with a sharp pull that rattled the pictures on the wall.

Stephanie sat motionless for a moment, then threw her pillow at the closed door with all her strength. It hit the door with a soft thud and slid to the floor.

She ran for the bathroom, keeping the sheet wrapped securely around her naked body even though she was alone.

The shower was hot and steamy. Under the water, she tried to turn her mind to what the new day would hold in her search, but her mind was filled with images of Elliot; in his towel, slicking his wet hair back into place, slipping into his jeans. It occurred to her that he'd put them on over his bare skin.

She turned to face the shower, inclined her head forward and let the water stream through, rinsing the last of the lather down the drain. She stood that way for a long time, thinking about the period of time she couldn't remember ("I undressed you, and put you to bed . . ."). Then she turned the water off and stepped out onto the cool tile floor.

She dressed quickly in a simple wrap skirt and a cool blouse. She slipped on a pair of comfortable walking shoes. There was a sharp knock at the door. Without thinking, Stephanie took the safety chain off, and was about to open the door when she remembered Elliot's warning. She secured the chain again, then opened the door the three inches it permitted.

"You kept the chain on. Good." Elliot's blue eyes regarded her with cool intensity through the small opening. "How about some breakfast while we plan our next move?"

"Sounds great to me." Stephanie closed the door briefly to unhook the chain, picked up her purse, and joined Elliot in the hall. He was wearing the worn jeans he'd put on in her room this morning, with a bright cobalt-blue polo shirt.

The walked silently to a small cafe three blocks from the hotel. They sat at a table for two on a patio facing the quiet side street. The smell of fresh, dark coffee blended with the salty smell of the nearby ocean.

A cruise ship had come into port late last night, and the first wave of passengers were leaving the launches and filling the streets of George Town for serious shopping. Soon the quiet town would be mobbed for a few hours, then the passengers would return to the ship, and the town would quiet down again.

Their waitress was an attractive young blond wearing white shorts and a tight T-shirt, about nineteen, Stephanie guessed. She was American, and she reminded Stephanie of the young girls she often saw on the beach back home. She brought them menus and coffee, openly staring at Elliot. She gave him a wink and left them to decide on breakfast.

"Airhead," Stephanie muttered under her breath.

"What?" Elliot looked up from his menu.

"Our little waitress. She looks like half the girls in Newport Beach. Probably has a rich daddy who's begging her to come back home and go to college so she can find a suitable husband to take her off his hands. She'll have fun here in the Caymans, then go back home when she's tired of it." Stephanie tried her coffee, but it was too hot to drink.

Elliot looked at Stephanie with surprise. "What makes you so angry about that?"

"I'm sorry. I don't mean to sound angry." Stephanie was shocked at how easily Elliot could read her. His directness inspired honesty in return. "My father deserted my mother while she was pregnant with me. It made things pretty tough for the two of us. I've worked very hard to get as far as I've gotten, and I guess sometimes I resent people that have had everything handed to them and don't appreciate it."

Stephanie realized with surprise that she had never stated her feelings about that early part of her life so clearly before, not even to herself.

Elliot's eyes were distant a moment, then he answered. "I understand feelings like that. Sometimes I think the only way anyone ever appreciates their own good fortune is to lose it." Stephanie wondered what had happened to Elliot that clouded his eyes with the memory.

The waitress came back for their order. Stephanie ordered a poached egg and dry wheat toast. The waitress took Stephanie's order, then turned her attention to Elliot. She brushed up lightly against Elliot when she reached across the table for his menu. Elliot smiled and laughed. Stephanie burned with irritation.

Probably just his type, she thought with disgust. Stephanie realized that Elliot was looking at her quizzically.

"What's the matter with you? Get up on the wrong side of the bed this morning?" He cocked a thick eyebrow at her suggestively. He was leaning back in his chair, one denim-clad leg crossed jauntily over the other. Stephanie saw the lanky cords of his thighs moving under the worn fabric. Both the breadth of his chest and the narrowness of his waist were emphasized by the thin cotton of his shirt. She remembered with agonizing clarity how hard that torso was to touch. She shook her head to clear the thought away.

"I'm sorry. I just don't like women who throw themselves at men. I think it's degrading." Hearing herself, she realized she sounded like some prissy virgin. Damn it, Elliot always seemed to get her flustered, to make her say things she didn't intend to!

Elliot assumed a look of pretended innocence. "You mean our little waitress? I don't know what you mean! I guess I just don't notice those kind of women." Elliot's eyes sparkled.

Stephanie bit back her sarcastic reply as the waitress appeared with their breakfast. Elliot continued to give Stephanie his look of exaggerated wide-eyed innocence as the waitress fussed over him, pouring more coffee, and offering to get him anything—with a significant wink—else he wanted. Stephanie's irritation vanished as Elliot shared the joke silently between them. When the waitress finally left, Stephanie began to giggle helplessly.

Elliot gave her a stern look. "Good service, madam, is certainly not a laughing matter." They both dissolved with laughter. "No, I'm serious!" Elliot insisted. "That girl has found her calling in the hospitality industry! She knows how important it is to keep the customer satisfied!"

Stephanie wiped the tears of laughter from her eyes. It felt good to laugh. It felt good to feel good.

For this moment, it seemed so pleasant, so normal, to be sitting here with Elliot, laughing over breakfast. She wanted to freeze the moment in her mind and hold on to it, to forget the pain and fears of the last few days and just keep drinking coffee and laughing with Elliot forever.

She looked at him, leaning back in his chair, finishing his coffee. He seemed younger this morning, fresher, not the jaded, worldly attorney who had strode into her office only a few days ago. His thick hair was tousled by the breeze, and his tan had deepened, making his eyes glow even more brightly. He was a beautiful man, no question about it. Stephanie wondered how many women had shared that thought.

Elliot sat up straight and put his coffee cup down suddenly, making a loud clink on the saucer. He wasn't looking at Stephanie now, but somewhere beyond her.

"What is it?" Stephanie felt the relaxation drain out of her in an instant.

"Don't move. Don't turn around. Just keep looking at me."

"Elliot—"

"Finish your coffee." He picked up his cup again and leaned back in his chair, but his body was tense, ready to react, and his eyes remained focused on a spot somewhere behind Stephanie.

A dirty white van drove slowly by the cafe. Elliot didn't turn his head as it passed. Stephanie kept her face toward Elliot, trying to watch the van out of the corner of her eye, but couldn't make out the driver. The van turned at the corner and passed out of sight.

Elliot stood up. "Let's go." He dropped some money on the table, but instead of heading toward the street, he grabbed Stephanie by the hand and pulled her into the greasy warmth of the kitchen, past the surprised cook, and found the small door in the back. Elliot pushed against the door, but it was locked.

"Elliot, what . . ."

"Come on." In a moment, he found the deadbolt and flipped it open. He jerked open the door, quickly looked both ways, and hustled them both out into a narrow alley. Elliot pressed Stephanie back against the rough brick of the building with a massive forearm. The white van drove by, hit its brakes with a screech, and pulled back far enough to make the sharp turn into the alley. It roared down the alley toward them.

Elliot's hand found the knob on the door to the kitchen. He twisted it, but it wouldn't open. He pounded on the door with his fist. Stephanie looked in terror from Elliot to the van bearing down on them. The morning sun was glaring on the windshield, making it a huge blank eye.

The door flew open, and Elliot shoved Stephanie into the kitchen, where she collided with the confused waitress. The tray of dirty dishes the waitress was carrying crashed to the floor in a slippery pile. Elliot grabbed Stephanie's arm and hustled her around the mess on the floor. The roar of the van's engine was cut by the slam of the door.

They went through the tiny kitchen in an instant. A few seconds later, they dodged the tables that stood in their way, and jumped the low railing separating the cafe from the street.

Within thirty seconds, Elliot and Stephanie were part of the huge anonymous crowd of cruise ship passengers that now filled the streets, determined to find enough bargains to sustain them until the next port of call.

TWELVE

Stephanie was surrounded by a colorful blur of humanity. Old people, teenagers, honeymooners, singles, families with children, all dressed in the bright, carefree outfits of vacation. They swirled and flowed around her, laden with bags and packages, moving purposefully from one shop to another in the square, in search of the duty-free riches of Cayman; English china, British woolens, French perfumes, and Irish linens and crystal.

She might have been swept away in the vivid wave, drowned in a sea of madras and splashy tropical prints, but Elliot was holding firmly to her hand, skillfully maneuvering them through the crowd. Several times Stephanie was certain they would collide with a tourist struggling under a huge load of packages, but Elliot would change direction at the last moment and avoid disaster. They stopped suddenly in front of a shop window displaying jewelry made from rare black coral.

"Looks like an interesting collection, darling. Let's take a look." Elliot took Stephanie's arm firmly.

"Elliot, I don't . . ." she protested in confusion.

"No, dearest, I insist. I want to buy you something really special to wear to the captain's party tonight." He looked directly into her eyes. "Let's go in. Right now."

She got the message. "Alright."

Inside the shop was a stunning array of beautiful things, not only jewlery, but nautical antiques and gold coins recovered from shipwrecks.

Elliot pulled her to the display case at the very rear of the shop. As they looked at several dramatic necklaces, Elliot kept one arm around her waist, and Stephanie could feel the tension in Elliot's body where he was pressed close to her as he continued the charade.

"Now, that one would look good with your short black dress; you know, the Halston." Elliot was watching the front door carefully. The sales woman was finishing with another customer and gestured that she would be with them in a moment. "Don't you think so."

"Ah, yes, the Halston; oh, yes, definitely." Were they being followed? Stephanie's heart was still pounding from their narrow escape from the van, and now she felt its beating even more strongly.

The crowds outside were growing bigger now; Stephanie remembered having heard that on certain weekdays as many as four cruise ships were in port at the same time. Several new customers entered the store. Another sales woman emerged from the backroom to assist with the sudden rush.

"Can I help you?" The sales woman who gestured to them earlier smiled thinly and regarded them skeptically over her chic glasses.

Elliot smiled warmly. "You've so many beautiful things, I think we need to browse for a while." He looked at Stephanie. "My wife isn't one to make a quick decision, are you, dear?" Stephanie nodded silently.

The sales woman wrinkled her nose with suspicion, and patted her tight bun of grey hair. "Certainly. Take as much time as you like. I'll be right here if you want anything." She moved on to assist an elderly couple looking at watches.

They moved on to another case containing silver Pieces of Eight and gold ducats, displayed dramatically on a swirl of thick midnight blue velvet. On the wall behind the case was a large modern map of the Caribbean, with colored push-pins stuck in various places. The push-pins marked the locations of the shipwrecks that the different coins in the case had been recovered from.

Stephanie examined the map while Elliot pretended a great interest in the coins. Something was gnawing at her brain. She crossed behind the glass case to get closer to the map. Stephanie felt something was here, something that the orderly, logical part of her mind would recognize, if only she could calm down and let that part of herself work for her. What was it?

Blotches, irregular blotches of color representing the land masses floating on a flat blue surface that was the Caribbean. Names of places and vital statistics in plain black type. Lines and numbers for navigation. Lines and numbers. Latitude and longitude.

In a blinding instant, she knew the answer. They had been wrong from the beginning! The number in the computer at Leo's wasn't a bank account number, or anything like that at all! It was a place. A precise location. Find that location, and they would find Leo! She was certain of that.

Stephanie's mouth was dust dry. She looked around for Elliot, but he had made his way around to the display case near the front door. She knew it wasn't the jewelry that had led him there. He was watching for something.

She dug in her purse for the number. She needn't have looked for it; when she found the slip of paper she realized she had recalled it perfectly from memory. 17–53–52/87–58–48. Stephanie checked quickly around the shop. No one seemed to be paying any attention to her. She leaned in close to the map.

She found the latitudinal line first, bisecting the map near its mid-point. It only took her a minute more to find its longitudinal counterpart and follow it down to where the two intersected. She pinpointed the spot with her trembling finger.

To Stephanie's surprise, her finger wasn't in the Caymans at all, but about five hundred miles to the west. With the limited information on this map, she could only approximate, but the coordinates seemed to fall on the Central American land mass, below the Yucatan Peninsula. She squinted to read the tiny letters. BELIZE.

"Well, dearest, if you haven't found anything here to spend my hard-earned salary on, I guess we'll have to try elsewhere." Stephanie jumped at the sound of Elliot's voice at her ear. "Looks like the coast is clear," he added under his breath.

"Elliot, we've made a big mistake." Stephanie fought to keep her voice low.

"You just now figured that out?" he took her arm. "Let's go." he started to steer her toward the door.

"Elliot, that's not what I mean. I'm talking about Leo." Elliot stopped abruptly. In her excitement, Stephanie spoke more loudly than she had intended. She became aware that while she'd been studying the map, most of the other customers had filtered out, and that they were now alone in the shop with the two sales women and a fat middle-aged American man who was looking at them curiously.

Stephanie shifted gears instantly. "I mean, I just don't think a large will be big enough. We should have gotten the extra-large." She gave a large sigh. "Please, can we go back to the boat? I'm so tired of shopping," she said, using her best impression of a spoiled-rich-wife whine.

"Yes, dear." Elliot escorted her out the door. They walked the two blocks to the wall overlooking the harbor before either one spoke. The morning sun glittered on the surface of the water.

"Damn it, Elliot, we've been looking in the wrong country!" Stephanie could barely contain her excitement.

Elliot gave a snort. "What do you mean, the wrong country? Maybe we haven't found him yet, but it sure as hell looks like somebody's been able to find us, right here in Cayman! I don't know who was in the van, but they definitely were looking for us, and probably still are."

"Elliot, you've got to listen to me. We made a wrong assumption right from the start. Do you know where Belize is?"

"Somewhere in Central America. What are you talking about?" Elliot looked at her as if she had suddenly started speaking another language.

Stephanie quickly explained what she'd found on the map. To her surprise, Elliot listened all the way through without interruption. When she finished, he was silent for a moment. She could see the wheels of his brain working.

"How much do you know about longitude and latitude anyway?" Elliot was surprisingly subdued.

"Very little," confessed Stephanie. "But Leo was an expert sailor, and he knew everything about navigation. All I know is what he tried to teach me the couple of times we went out on his boat in Newport. It wasn't much."

"I can handle a boat pretty well myself. If your idea is right, we've got to find a more detailed map. Leo's given us coordinates with hours, minutes, and seconds, so we should be able to pinpoint the spot within a very narrow range."

"Where can we find a map?" Stephanie's sense of urgency was growing.

"The dive shop should have what we need. Let's give it a try."

Billy was alone in the dive shop this morning. He appeared to be suffering from a severe hangover. He looked grateful to be spending this morning on dry land.

"Hi, I'm Stephanie. Remember me?"

"Sure, I remember you." Billy eyed Elliot cautiously. "You never said good-bye yesterday."

"Sorry. I was, ah, meeting someone." She looked to Elliot for help, but he didn't come to her rescue. "This is Elliot, a friend of mine." The two men shook hands.

"I was hoping you could help us out." Stephanie launched into the elaborate story she had prepared, about a sailing trip they were contemplating, but it was unnecessary. Billy was more interested in nursing his hangover undisturbed than their reasons for looking over his charts, and he soon spread everything out on the countertop for them to examine.

"I gotta go fill tanks." Billy yawned loudly. "You guys watch the shop for me, okay?" Billy headed down to the compressor room, rubbing his aching head. The door banged shut behind him, and the little bell attached to the top of the door jangled brightly.

Stephanie and Elliot shuffled through the stacks of nautical charts showing the Caribbean in hundreds of different sections and scales. They searched for several minutes without speaking.

"Here it is!" Elliot circled a spot on one of the charts. He was silent for a moment. "It's not on the mainland at all. In fact, it's not land at all. Take a look." Elliot threw down his pencil and walked to the window. "Apparently Martindale's not quite the hotshot navigator you said he was." He crossed his arms and stared silently out to sea.

Stephanie looked at the mark Elliot made. The coordinates intersected in the ocean, right in the midst of a mass of tiny coral islands off the coast of Belize. Little, uninhabited coral specks. Only the larger ones had names. Most were unnamed even on the detailed charts.

"It must be one of these islands. He probably had to make the best guess he could."

Elliot didn't turn from the window. When he spoke, his voice was flat and emotionless. "There's no point in continuing with this search any longer. We'd never have time to reach even half those islands."

Stephanie felt her stomach become an empty pit. She touched the spot on the map again, trying to make it real to herself. She had been so sure that this would be the solution, that they would be able to find Leo and this nightmare would come to an end! What was today? Thursday? Elliot had to have her back to California by eight o'clock Monday morning, to face the judge who had given her permission for this useless journey. Tears filled her eyes, and she brushed them away, silently damning herself for her weakness.

Elliot's hands were on her shoulders. He turned her around to face him. She kept her face down, unwilling to look at him, unable to meet his eyes and see the reproach for her stupidity, her weakness, her helplessness in this situation. She didn't want him to see her like this.

Elliot's hands found her face and turned it gently up toward him. He carefully wiped away a single tear making its way down her cheek with the rough tip of his forefinger. His tenderness moved her more than she thought she could bear. The lump of tears that blocked her throat began to dissolve in a cleansing flood of release.

He gently eased her head to rest against his cheek. Her tears came hot and fast. With one large hand, he cradled her head against him; the other found the small of her back and pulled her firmly to him. Stephanie locked her arms behind him and pressed herself tightly against him, wanting to feel his strength, his power, his comfort more completely. She felt her body mold to his, drawing from him, taking from him.

She remembered this morning and how he looked standing in her room, nearly naked, his taut chest glistening wet. Her fingers dipped below the collar of his shirt to feel his skin, the warmth of the strong column of his neck.

Elliot's lips, which had first touched her so softly, so carefully, now were kissing around her mouth quickly, firmly. She opened to him, drawing him in, drawing in his strength.

The taste of his mouth was warm and mellow, spicy and comforting. Stephanie's eyes were closed, and she existed only in the reality of this moment. Elliot's arms holding her; Elliot's mouth filling her, releasing himself to her.

His hand cupped her right breast in a natural, almost unconscious gesture. Stephanie felt an electric surge of aching desire. She leaned into his touch, somehow both rough and gentle at the same time, an exquisite mixture of desire and tenderness.

The sudden jangle of the little bells above the door broke their union. They jumped apart like high school kids interrupted in a steamed-up car. Stephanie's checks were burning. Elliot looked absolutely sheepish.

"Sorry." Billy stood in the shop doorway, looking more flustered than the two of them did. "I guess I should have knocked or something. . . ." He put down the two scuba tanks he was carrying. "Did you find what you needed?"

"Yes, we sure did." Elliot picked up the top chart from the stack. "Do you mind if we take this one with us?"

"No problem. It's on the house." Billy put the rest of the stack away in a drawer behind the counter.

"Thanks for your help, Billy." Elliot rolled up the chart carefully. "We'd better get moving, Stephanie." He opened the door. Stephanie picked up her purse, and moved slowly to the door. She'd been dropped back into reality with an unpleasant jolt.

_____ THIRTEEN _____

When they crossed the runway and stepped into the terminal at Belize International Airport, Stephanie felt they had stepped out of the modern world into a Humphrey Bogart movie. The afternoon air was warm and dense with humidity in the primitive two-room building. Frosted louver windows were open to the outside, and ceiling fans turned slowly overhead, but they did little to provide relief from the oppressive jungle air. The cream colored, fly-specked walls were decorated with simple, hand-lettered signs advertising local restaurants and hotels. The terminal had few travellers, mostly native Belizeans returning home. There were no Americans.

"Quite a shock after the Caymans," Elliot said. Stephanie nodded in agreement. In Cayman, in spite of the natural beauty and simplicity of the islands, she had never felt very far removed from the modern world as she knew it. Belize, however, was like a journey into a strange past she didn't recognize. Stephanie knew that Belize, like the Cayman Islands, had once been one of Great Britain's colonies. Unlike Cayman, however, which had remained fiercely loyal to the Crown and rejected independence, Belize had finally become an independent nation less than ten years ago.

A uniformed official dozed behind a small, battered desk marked CUSTOMS. He looked up sleepily as Stephanie and Elliot approached the desk and presented their passports. The official took a long time to review their passports, and even longer to find his rubber stamp and worn ink pad. Stephanie felt a trickle of sweat run down between her shoulder blades. Her blouse clung moistly to the underside of her breasts. Elliot shifted his carry-on bag to his other shoulder and touched her arm lightly. The easy familiarity of his touch reassured her. She covered his hand with her own and squeezed gently, holding it tight to her arm.

Finally, the customs man finished lazily stamping their passports. He handed Elliot's back to him wordlessly. He examined Stephanie's passport photo one final time, then gave her a long provocative stare. He smiled broadly at her, still holding on to her passport, his smile flashing white and gold in his dark face.

"Welcome to Belize, Miss Robinson." He handed her passport back to Stephanie, allowing his fingers to touch her hand in exchange.

The touch of his hand sent a shiver through her body, but Stephanie managed a wan smile back. The humidity was giving her a dull ache in the middle of her forehead. She was grateful when Elliot put a hand on her arm and steered her toward the door leading outside.

The rest of the morning in Cayman had passed in a flush of nervous preparation. They caught a cab outside the dive shop for the short drive back to the hotel. Neither one of them mentioned what Billy had interrupted. Stephanie's heart was pounding, and she told herself it was because of the excitement of the new lead they were following. Finding Leo was all that mattered. Then why did she keep thinking of Elliot's mouth on her's, and his hand at her breast?

Back at the hotel, Elliot made the arrangements for the short flight from George Town to Belize City on the telephone in Stephanie's room, while she packed the few clothes she'd brought with her. He sat on the edge of the bed, watching her move about the small room as he waited on hold, the phone held casually to his ear. He leaned back against the headboard and swung his long legs up onto the bed as he waited. Elliot had a natural, graceful way of moving; he moved like a man who was the master of his body. It was a pleasure to watch him do the simplest task.

It didn't take long for Elliot to pack. Stephanie leaned against the door of his room, her small suitcase at her side, as he swept his clothes into a dark green duffle bag and grabbed the leather shaving kit out of the bathroom. The room smelled faintly of Elliot's after-shave.

Stephanie tried to imagine what his bedroom at home looked like. Was it messy? Utilitarian and neat? Sophisticated? She really knew very little about this man. It was as if each of their lives had started at that first meeting in her office; she felt an odd sense of intimacy in his presence now. It wasn't a comfortable feeling at all. She felt disoriented, almost light-headed. She reached down to check for her suitcase, even though she had put it down only moments before.

Elliot took a last quick look around the room. "Guess that's everything." He dropped the duffle bag on the bed, still neatly made up since he'd never slept in it last night. He turned and looked at Stephanie, propped up against the door. Damn, but she looked great. Her practical travelling clothes couldn't conceal her body from his eyes. He remembered every detail from last night. Concerned as he had been to get her dry and snugly into bed, his eyes had drunk in her body's perfection as he had undressed her and toweled her dry. Those long legs, now clad in no-nonsense khaki, were strong and graceful, swelling to a luscious fullness at her hips. The simple navy-blue polo shirt she wore revealed the curves of her full breasts. Elliot ached with the memory of her large rose-dark nipples puckering as he'd gently toweled her dry.

She looked so vulnerable, so trusting, leaning against the door as she waited for him to finish. Elliot felt his chest tighten with tenderness. She needed to be taken care of. She hadn't done anything to deserve this mess, but she'd wound up right in the middle of it, and held up damn well, too.

"You look like you're getting ready to run away from home."

"Sounds like a good idea. You want to come, too?" Stephanie smiled at him, and Elliot was overwhelmed with the desire to protect her from what could be ahead.

He crossed to her in two quick steps and took her chin gently in one hand, and kissed her gently, just once. Her hands flew from her sides to touch his arms. He forced himself to end the kiss. "Time to leave this gracious establishment, Ms. Robinson. We've got a plane to catch." He kissed her again, quickly, then picked up their bags.

To Stephanie's relief, Elliot took care of checking out for both of them. The desk clerk had on a clean shirt today, but the same sour expression. Stephanie stood at the farthest corner of the lobby away from him and ignored his frequent leers in her direction. *I'd be absolutely no good at having an illicit hotel rendezvous*, she thought to herself.

They rode to the airport in silence. Elliot seemed lost in his own thoughts, so Stephanie stared out the window as the cab driver drove them to the airport at a slow, careful pace. They had allowed plenty of time to catch the flight, but Stephanie was nervous. She studied Elliot surreptitiously during the ride. His face didn't show the nervousness and excitement that she was feeling. How could he be so damn cool? She envied that; as a matter of fact, before this bizarre adventure had begun, she had always thought of herself as cool, controlled; a thinker, rather than a feeler. It had been essential to her success in a man's world. She sure as hell didn't feel cool right now! And as far as thinking and feeling went, she'd never felt so many conflicting, crazy emotions in a few short days in her entire life, and nothing could change that. Something was happening to Stephanie that she hadn't ever experienced before. For the first time in her life, she wanted something with all her heart that didn't make sense, that wasn't logical; something that was overriding all the "shoulds" and "musts" and "have tos" that had always guided her. She wanted Elliot.

The flight to Belize City was easy. The small commuter plane had seats to accommodate only eighteen passengers, and they took the last seats in the rear of the plane. Up to now, Stephanie had deliberately avoided the subject of what they would do once they reached Belize. It had been enough that they weren't giving up, that there was still a chance to find Leo before their alloted time was up. Finally, she couldn't wait any longer.

"What are we going to do once we get there? We could hire someone to take us out in a boat, but Leo's coordinates don't seem to be quite right anyway.'' Her words spilled out in a sudden burst of uncertainty.

Elliot was thoughtful. "First of all, we don't really know if Leo's information is right or not. There are hundreds of islands in that area, and not all of them are on the charts.'' His eyes studied her face intently. "In any case, I don't think we should hire a boat to take us out there. If we go asking around to hire someone, we might as well tell the whole country. Something tells me we haven't seen the last of our friends from Cayman.''

Stephanie felt like her ribs were being pressed against, making it difficult to breathe.''Then what are we going to do? What's the point if we can't get out to those islands?''

"We're going to get out there, alright. But we've got to do it without attracting attention. I've already looked into chartering a sailboat big enough for us to live aboard.''

"A sailboat? Why?''

"Because, what could be more innocent than a nice young couple enjoying a romantic honeymoon all alone on a sailboat?''

"Honeymoon?'' A curious lump had formed in Stephanie's throat. She tried to swallow it away, but it stubbornly refused to budge.

Elliot's blue gaze locked hers. "That's right. A couple on their honeymoon, all alone, enjoying this little corner of the Caribbean. That way, we can go wherever we like, really check out that area from Leo's message, without attracting any undue attention.''

"But who's going to sail this boat?'' Stephanie knitted her thick brows in confusion.

"Don't worry, Ms. Robinson. I am a man of many talents.''

The sound of the engines changed, and the plane began its descent toward the dark blue-green jungles surrounding Belize City.

Elliot pushed open the door leading outside, and the wet smell of the jungle was like walking into a soft damp mattress. On a rusty pole was a weathered metal sign that read "TAXI," and beside it five cars of inde-terminate older vintage were parked behind each other. The drivers formed a loose circle around the man sitting on the hood of the first old station wagon in line, who was in the middle of telling what sounded like a very raw joke. He finished the punch line with a broad ges-ture and a rude noise. The other men dissolved into a raucous laughter.

Elliot and Stephanie waited for a few moments to be noticed, but the men were too engrossed in their private conversation to notice the travellers. Elliot dropped his duffle bag to the ground with a deliberate thud, and the men paused in their conversation. They slowly exam-ined Stephanie with appreciative eyes and exchanged glances laden with meaning between one another. The man who had been telling the joke finally approached.

"Taxi?" He spoke to Elliot, but kept his eyes on Stephanie. In spite of her practical khaki slacks and cotton polo shirt, his brazen gaze made her feel as if she were wearing something daring and provocative. She crossed her arms over her chest in a unconscious gesture of modesty. Elliot sensed her discomfort, and put a proprietary arm around her waist. Elliot nodded silently, and the driver opened the door for them.

Stephanie got into the back seat of the taxi. The worn vinyl of the backseat had been repaired in so many places with layers of duct tape that it was hard to distin-guish the original color. Elliot slid in next to her, and slammed the door solidly. He sat close to her, and Stephanie felt the strength of his hard thigh pressed up against her leg. She was grateful for Elliot's comforting presence. This place frightened her.

"Please take us to the waterfront." The driver nodded to Elliot in the rearview mirror and started the station wagon's engine. Stephanie was grateful that Belize, like the Cayman Islands, was primarily an English-speaking country. At least they didn't have to deal with a language barrier.

The driver pulled out of the airport lot and turned onto a narrow but paved highway. The road cut through heavy vegetation growing on both sides. Something big and green scampered across the road in front of them, barely avoiding the taxi's tires. Stephanie gasped involuntarily.

"Just an iguana, Miss." The driver laughed, enjoying Stephanie's fright. She felt herself turning red with embarrassment. Elliot laid his warm hand on her knee in silent understanding.

The humidity became less oppressive as they neared the ocean. The sleepy waterfront area came into view, and Stephanie could see two small hotels. Docked nearby were three large live-aboard dive boats, about seventy-five feet in length, ready to take groups of scuba divers out for a week or more of diving on the famous Barrier Reef. The airline magazine had told Stephanie that the reef was second in size only to Australia's Great Barrier Reef.

Elliot directed the driver to continue past the hotels to the far end of the marina. He dropped them off in front of the small office on the dock. The sun-bleached sign above the door read PARADISE YACHT CHARTERS.

Inside the tiny office, a grizzled old man that Steph-

anie guessed to be about seventy was smoking a cigarette and pouring over ledgers. A faded red bandana
covered his head, tied with a rakish knot. He looked
up as they entered, but didn't speak at first. He crushed
out his unfiltered cigarette with yellow, tobacco-stained
fingers.

"You the McKeons?" The man sat back in his
wooden swivel chair and lit another cigarette. Stephanie
noticed that he wasn't wearing his dentures, and his
gums flashed pink when he spoke. His muddy brown
eyes evaluated them in a slow sweep.

"Yes. I called early this morning about a charter."
Elliot's large presence dominated the room. "Has the
boat been provisioned as I asked? My wife and I are
anxious to get underway."

"Yes, the *Windy Love* is all set to sail. But don't be
in such a hurry just yet. We're gonna have to check
you out, Mr. McKeon. We can't let just anybody take
one of our boats out alone. You said you didn't want
no captain." He looked at Elliot defiantly. "These are
tricky waters here on the reef. Better be a damn good
sailor."

Stephanie's heart was pounding. She didn't know
about Elliot, but she knew practically nothing about
sailing. As she'd told Elliot, she'd been out with Leo
a few times, but that was it. Could they handle a forty-
six foot boat on their own in these unfamiliar waters?

"That won't be a problem. I have my captain's
license." Stephanie tried hard to conceal her amazement. Elliot was full of surprises. He pulled a document
folder from his duffle bag. "This should be more than
enough."

The old man examined the papers with a critical eye.
Apparently satisfied, he grunted and pushed them back
across the desk to Elliot. He pulled out a contract on

a clipboard and handed it to Elliot to complete. He lit another cigarette without bothering to extinguish the one still smoldering in the ashtray. He turned his attention to Stephanie.

"So, it's your honeymoon, is it?" His words had a leering undertone to them. Stephanie nodded mutely. "Well, that's nice. It'll be real nice and private out there at sea." He took a long drag on his cigarette. "Now, you be sure and wear your suntan lotion; that is, if you ever get out of your cabin!" He laughed coarsely at his own joke, until Elliot looked at him pointedly, and the laugh turned into a hoarse, hacking cough.

Elliot put the clipboard down with a snap, then laughed with good humor. "OK, Gramps, show us to the *Windy Love*." He put his arm around Stephanie's waist. His big hand pinched playfully at her hip. "I can't wait too much longer."

The old man led them down the dock to the last boat that was tied at the very end. Stephanie thought it was the prettiest sailboat she'd ever seen. Its graceful wood glowed warmly from years of polishing. The old man gave them a quick tour.

The open-air cockpit was at the mid-point of the boat, comfortably padded bench seats surrounding the bright brass wheel and compass. Down several short steps, directly below was the main salon and galley. The salon glinted with bright brass and polished wood. The galley was tiny, but well organized. The old man gave them instructions on lighting the stove and keeping the refrigerator cold.

A short hall to the rear of the boat led to the main cabin, dominated by a large bed built into a polished wooden frame. The old man nudged Elliot and winked broadly at Stephanie. To her embarrassment, she blushed bright red. *Very funny*, she thought to herself, *the blushing bride*. What a performance. Elliot was playing his part, too, she noticed. He looked convincingly like a red-blooded male anxious to start enjoying his honeymoon, and his new bride. He was looking at her with a provocative gleam in his eye that caused her heart to turn over in her chest.

After a quick look at the bathroom—head, Elliot corrected her—they went back topside. The old man gave Elliot a quick rundown of the boat's rigging. Stephanie could tell the old man was still testing Elliot. Elliot passed with flying colors, answering all the questions posed to him with confidence. Finally, the old man seemed satisfied.

"Well, I guess that's about all you need to know. You still planning on heading out today?" The old man offered Stephanie a gnarled hand as she stepped back onto the dock.

"Yes, it's only four; we'll have good light for a couple of hours." The old man nodded in sage agreement and went back to the office for the key to the engine. Stephanie waited on the dock.

Elliot picked up their luggage and hopped back aboard. He disappeared into the cabin below. A moment later he emerged. He'd changed out of his jeans into a worn pair of white cotton shorts. His feet and chest were bare. Stephanie watched as he moved quickly about the boat, checking the rigging of the sails, familiarizing himself with the arrangement of the hardware. She couldn't take her eyes off the huge man moving so nimbly about the boat. Seeing him at work like this, she was struck by how natural he looked doing physical things. His large, powerful feet gripped the smooth surfaces of the deck with ease. His chest and arms were as deeply tanned as the handsome wood of the boat.

He knelt down to inspect the electric anchor winch, and the leg of his brief shorts pulled up high, exposing the bunching muscles of his thighs. Stephanie's own thighs tightened in involuntary response. His head was bent in concentration, and she noticed the powerful line of his neck where it melded with his broad shoulders. The image of her lips tracing that line rose unbidden in her mind.

"This should be all you need now." The old man appeared with the key. "Looks like you've already made yourself at home," he said when he saw Elliot. "How 'bout you, little lady? 'Bout time for you to change into your prettiest bikini, huh?" He laughed loudly. Stephanie said nothing. Elliot extended his hand to her, and she took it gratefully as she came aboard.

The engine started easily. "We'll motor out of the harbor, then get the feel of things once we're in open water." Stephanie and the old man freed the boat from its tie lines, and Elliot took the wheel. Within seconds, they were pulling smoothly away from the dock.

"Have a good time!" The old man waved from the dock, his braying laugh carrying across the widening space between them. Elliot motored slowly through the harbor. He stood at the wheel, while Stephanie sat on the cockpit bench to his right. He handled the wheel with a light, comfortable touch that was a pleasure to watch. The muscles in his arms and shoulders played fluidly under his bronzed skin. Stephanie was getting warm in her long pants, and so she went below to change into her swimsuit, a discreet navy one-piece. When she came back up the ladder, Elliot looked her over with obvious approval.

"Very nice. Did you buy that for the honeymoon?"

His smile was gently teasing, but his eyes had a sharp glint that cut right to her heart. She tried to come back with a clever retort, but her wits failed her. She returned to her seat in the cockpit. Elliot was guiding the boat out of the harbor into the open sea.

"Where are you going?" Her mouth was dry. Having Elliot so close to her was starting to play havoc with her senses. She admired the taut surface of his belly, which was right at her eye level. The light dusting of dark hair became darker where it disappeared below the waistband of his shorts.

"Not very far; not tonight. There's a little island that we can reach in about two hours if we stay under motor. The chart shows an easy anchorage there. We can spend the night and get an early start out to the reef tomorrow."

"Is there anything you want me to do for you?" She winced at the unintentional innuendo of the question.

"Not right now. Just relax and enjoy the trip."

Stephanie stretched out on the warm cockpit seat. She closed her eyes against the afternoon sun. She couldn't shake the consciousness of Elliot so close to her. The warm, spicy scent of his body wafted over her. Without thinking, she inhaled deeply, filling her nostrils with the tantalizing essence. Even with her eyes closed, she could see him as looked right now at the wheel, with the sun gleaming on his smooth tanned skin and reflecting brightly in his glossy hair. She opened her eyes.

"How come you know so much about boats?" She pulled herself up to lean on her elbow.

"I started sailing when I was a kid. Then, when I needed a job my last couple years in college, I started doing boat maintenance and working crew for a sailing club. By the time I finished law school, I had enough hours of experience to get my captain's license."

"That sound's a lot more interesting than my college job. I worked in the university's copy center. I can still smell the toner from those machines." She wrinkled her nose in distaste. "Did you work your way through school?"

A darkness clouded the bright blue of his eyes. "I was on an athletic scholarship the first few years, but that didn't work out, so after that I was on my own." The small lines around his smooth mouth deepened slightly.

Stephanie felt him withdrawing from their conversation, his mind moving to another time and place. She was sorry the comfortable intimacy of the moment had been broken. She silently scanned the horizon. "Is that where we're spending tonight?" The island was tiny, a small pink coral speck. She'd been aware of its outline on the horizon since they'd left the harbor, but suddenly it appeared to be much closer. She could make out a slim crescent-shaped beach bordered by palms, curving around a small cove.

"That's it. There should be an easy anchorage in the cove off that little beach." He leaned to the left for a better view. "Here, hold the wheel steady." Stephanie took the wheel with trepidation. The brass was warm from Elliot's hands. Elliot stepped out of the cockpit with one powerful step and quickly made his way forward to the stern of the boat. He surveyed the island from his position, then was back at her side. He took the wheel back from Stephanie.

Fifteen minutes later they were entering the protected little cove, and the wake from the boat sent a series of wavelets shimmering across the surface of the water to lap at the sand. Elliot brought the boat around in a smooth circle, put the engine in neutral, and in an instant released the anchor from its winch at the bow. He returned to the wheel. When he felt the anchor grip securely in the shallow bottom, he shut off the engine.

The sudden silence was overwhelming. The disturbance of their boat's wake gradually faded until the surface of the cove was smooth and glasslike again. The boat drifted gently back, pulling against the anchor line until it found its resting place. Stephanie went to the edge of the deck to look down. The water was a translucent blue-green, revealing a wealth of marine creatures in the coral heads below. Stephanie's gaze swept over the white beach. She couldn't discern what was beyond the grove of palms. A light breeze carried the scent of the island to her, light, tangy, fresh; yet ancient and eternal as well.

She turned around to Elliot, but he wasn't looking at the island. He was looking at her, slowly moving his gaze down her body, lingering over the curves of her breasts. She felt his gaze on her like sunlight, warming her skin wherever it touched her. His eyes followed the long line of her legs, then moved back to her face. She met his eyes. They were a deeper shade than she'd seen them before, the centers reflecting the darkening waters surrounding the boat.

"It's a lovely spot." Stephanie's voice sounded unexpectedly rough and throaty, as if she'd just awakened after a long sleep and hadn't spoken yet.

"Yes. It's as if we were the only two people to have ever been in this place."

Stephanie forced herself to turn away from Elliot, to unlock herself from those eyes. "It should be a terrific sunset." The sun was moving slowly toward its inevitable plunge into the Caribbean. The horizon line shimmered in the distance.

She turned back just as Elliot was emerging from the galley below. She hadn't heard him descend. He was carrying two crystal-clear acrylic wine glasses, filled with a liquid the color of mown hay. He put one in her hand. It was icy cold, and little droplets of moisture were forming on the outside.

"I thought a toast was in order." He patted the cockpit seat beside him. She sat down, and her leg brushed up slightly against his scarred knee. "To fair weather, kind seas, and good sailing." They clinked their glasses together and Stephanie sipped her wine. The cool Chardonnay felt good after having the salty taste of the sea in her mouth all afternoon. It ran down her throat in a soothing stream.

She studied Elliot over the rim of her wineglass. He was leaning back, his feet propped up on the base of the wheel rising from the deck. He'd pulled on a faded T-shirt that didn't conceal the hardness of his torso beneath. He was gazing out toward the setting sun. The small lines around his mouth and eyes smoothed out.

"I have a toast, too." Stephanie raised her glass, and waited for Elliot to follow. A small lump caught in her throat, but she swallowed it away. "To finding Leo." They clinked glasses gently. Elliot put his large, warm hand on her leg. The rough skin of his palm tingled against the skin of her bare thigh.

"We will, Stephanie. I swear to God we will." His eyes smoldered darkly in his tan face. "And we're not going back until we do."

_____ FOURTEEN _____

Stephanie grasped the lifelines and gazed into the burning sunset. The fiery ball descended smoothly into the blue water of the Caribbean. Elliot had gone below to return their empty wineglasses to the galley.

Two strong hands touched the small of her back, powerful fingers spreading out to encircle her waist and fan out over the swelling of her hips. Two powerful thumbs began a gentle kneading of the tight muscles of Stephanie's lower back, each firmly tracing either side of the ridge of her spine.

Stephanie felt warm breath at the nape of her neck, gently stirring the tiny down at her hairline. Elliot's strong thumbs kept up their firm pressure, and the knots of tension began to dissolve under their friction. As his hands slipped around her waist Elliot began to kiss her neck slowly, his lips lingering over the sensitive skin just below her ear.

Stephanie grasped the lifelines more tightly, and leaned back against Elliot's hard chest. Her bare back felt the muscles of his chest move as his hands slid caressingly up her stomach. The rough pads of his fingertips burned through the thin fabric of her swim suit. He caressed her in slow, languid strokes, starting at the slight curve of her stomach, his fingertips reaching a little higher each time.

His breath warmed her right ear, and his tongue began a gentle exploration of her earlobe, moving slowly up to lave inside the sensitive opening. Each touch sent a shivering ripple of electricity down her back.

The long stroking continued, each time stopping short of her breasts, which began to warm and swell with desire to be touched. When she thought she could wait no longer, his hands finally brushed up against them. Her held breath came out in a little involuntary burst of sound. He stroked the underside of her breasts with his fingertips, then smoothly circled her nipples with his index fingers. The soft peaks grew hard underneath his searching fingers and strained against the fabric of her suit. Elliot's large callused palms cupped her soft full breasts completely now, and she longed for him to release them, to touch their bare smoothness, to tease them with the feathery kisses that he was now bestowing on her bare shoulders.

The sun sank lower, until only a sliver of orange shone above the horizon. Stephanie felt Elliot's hand leave her breast to slowly peel down the right shoulder of her suit, then the left, gently pulling the snug fabric off her shoulders and down her body, freeing her breasts to him. His hands were hot against the bare skin. He gently teased her nipples into harder and harder peaks of pleasure with the light touch of his rough fingertips. Stephanie shifted, filling both his hands with the warm, swollen fullness of her breasts. Elliot moaned his appreciation wordlessly into her ear, gently massaging with his big palms.

She felt weak, as she leaned almost imperceptibly back. She felt the hardness of his thighs against her bottom, and the full strength of his desire was against her lower back. Her breath came faster, but Elliot was in no hurry. The sun slipped below the horizon.

"I think the sunset's over." His words seemed to come from far away, his voice a rough, dark sound that echoed deep within her body.

Stephanie let go of the lifelines and turned at last. His strong arms pressed her almost naked body to him. His mouth found hers, and his kiss filled her up in a way that was different from the kisses they'd shared before. As his tongue searched her mouth, Stephanie felt an eagerness, a need, a hunger that she knew had always been within her, but never emerged until this moment. She explored his shoulders, his neck, his chest, his body moving under the worn cotton of his T-shirt. She lifted his shirt and felt the ridged quadrants of his hard belly. Her hand strayed lower, and brushed the front of his worn shorts. Stephanie gasped slightly and pulled her hand away. Elliot's kisses became more intense, more filled with his growing need.

All of a sudden, Elliot broke away. He stepped back, keeping hold only of her right hand. He looked at her reverently in the dusky half-light, up and down. Stephanie suddenly felt shy over her near nakedness. She covered her breasts with her free arm.

Elliot reached out to take a strand of her hair in his hand, then put his arm around her neck and pulled Stephanie to him. He kissed her tenderly once more, then silently led her to the stairway leading to the cabin below.

Once in the main berth, Elliot cranked open the hatch over the bed. The boat was swaying very slightly, very serenely. Stephanie sat down on the bed. She found her voice.

"I feel at somewhat of a disadvantage, counselor. You still have all your clothes on."

"That's easily remedied," said Elliot. He pulled his shirt off in one smooth motion, his raised arms emphasizing the massive wedge of his torso. Elliot tossed the shirt aside and sat down beside Stephanie. As he kissed her, Stephanie found herself now the aggressor, pulling him to her. Her breasts now pressed against his bare skin for the first time. Her hands now wandered eagerly, shamelessly over his body. Her hands found his waist, his flat, hard stomach, and then the waistband of his shorts. She hooked her fingers in the worn elastic and raked them off in one motion. They were stretched out on the wonderful firmness of the bed. Stephanie lay on her back, Elliot covering her neck, her shoulders, her breasts with quick, eager kisses. Above her, the night sky was filling with stars, bright, crystalline in their clarity; Stephanie felt as if they were there just for her, tonight, this moment. Elliot's tireless kisses moved down her stomach. The gentle rocking motion of the boat became more pronounced.

Elliot was at her hips now, and with a gentle pull drew off her tank suit and tossed it away. His hands caressed the length of her legs, her hips, her thighs, her calves. His hands smoothly stroked the back of her knees, the inside of her thighs, her warm buttocks. Stephanie let a small moan escape her lips as Elliot finally slid his hand gently up her inner thigh, higher, higher, to touch her warmth, her center. His big hand gently cupped the nest of auburn curls at her thigh's juncture. Pleasure washed over her in waves, each breaking a little higher than the last.

Stephanie was ready for him, eager, waiting. She

drew Elliot up to her face to kiss him deeply. He entered her with a single slow stroke, and her body opened to receive him. As he drew her into his slow, even rhythm, Stephanie felt the motions of their love meld with the boat's gentle sway, to become part of the whole rhythm of the earth, the stars above her, the universe.

Her hands sought his muscular buttocks, and she urged him on, feeling her need grow greater with his own passionate desire for her. Stephanie's hips joined his as they encouraged each other, riding wave after wave, each higher and farther than the last, so high that Stephanie wondered if she was in danger of crashing down and drowning in the dangerous froth. But strangely, she felt no fear, and when it came, that last wave didn't send her crashing into the dark waters, but instead laid her gently on the sands of a golden, lovely beach, where she slumbered gently in the friendly tropical sun.

When Stephanie awoke, it was two hours later. The full moon had risen, and the stars were dimmed by its bright glow. She lay without moving, looking at the moon, trying to remember the dream she'd been having. Something to do with the ocean, waves, yes, and a beach . . . All at once, Stephanie became aware of another presence. She turned her head to the right and found herself almost nose-to-nose with Elliot, who was deep asleep. She realized her dream had not been a dream at all.

Stephanie eased herself out of bed, moving slowly to not awaken Elliot. Wrapping herself in a towel, she climbed the steps to the boat's deck. Her bare feet padded soundlessly on the brightly polished wooden surface. She made her way to the bow of the boat, and stood on the dolphin striker that projected out over the surface of the water.

The night was warm. The full moon was bright, and
as her eyes adjusted more to the night setting, Stephanie
could clearly see the outline of the little cove they were
anchored in, and the sand of the small crescent beach
surrounded by palm trees. It reminded Stephanie of the
beach in her dream. She thought of Elliot, sleeping
peacefully below her.

The water in the cove was calm, and the moon's
reflection shimmered slightly on the surface of the
water. Stephanie leaned back against the secure railing
of the dolphin striker and looked toward the beach.

So, it had finally happened. She and Elliot had made
love. She thought of him bursting into her office that
first morning; how long ago had it been? A week,
maybe—it seemed a lifetime ago.

It had been wonderful; no, incredible. She smiled in
the moonlight. No question about that—but what did it
mean in the light of the bizarre circumstances that had
brought them together? Falling in love with Elliot
would be a big mistake. Their relationship was its own
strange version of a shipboard romance, and she would
be a fool to believe it could ever be anything more than
that. But knowing that didn't change the feelings that
moved within her.

She'd been alone so long, fighting her own battles,
but never sharing the sweet victories or painful defeats
with anyone. She was used to the slightly hollow feeling that followed even the things she'd strived for the
hardest. She felt her own loneliness acutely, yet had
come to accept it as a fact of her life. Sometimes, late
at night, she wondered if she would always be alone.

But now, there was Elliot. Somehow, having him to
share this frightening time had made her feel that she
would survive. She would be alright. She wasn't alone.
Elliot was with her. They were in this together. But

when this time was over, and she was alone again, the hollow ache would return. Stephanie knew that it would be far worse than ever before.

A slight warm breeze moved in from the island. Against Stephanie's skin, the air felt relaxing, almost liquid. She dropped the towel that she had wrapped around herself, and let the soft tropical air caress her naked body. She closed her eyes and thought—*Just a minute, just for a few minutes of this peaceful night, and then I'll make my way back to my own bed. In the morning, Elliot and I will continue the search for Leo, and we'll pretend nothing has happened.*

When Stephanie opened her eyes a few moments later, she realized that she was no longer alone. Elliot was standing back by the mast, leaning against it, watching her. He was wearing only the cotton shorts she had taken off him earlier that evening. His chest was bare, and even in the moonlight the hard outline of his body was clear.

Suddenly aware of her nakedness, Stephanie grabbed her towel from the deck where it had fallen.

"How long have you been standing there?" she demanded.

Elliot's teeth flashed white in the moonlight.

"Long enough."

"You've got a lot of nerve sneaking up on a person like that." Stephanie tried to regain her dignity as she moved resolutely toward the steps to below deck. Elliot's strong arms stopped her halfway to her destination.

"Hold on a minute, what's the matter? It's not like we're strangers, right?" Elliot's blue eyes regarded her with gentle amusement.

"Let me go, Elliot!" Stephanie struggled against the strong grip he had, his two hands on her two shoulders.

She looked into his laughing face defiantly. "I was afraid something like this would happen."

"Something like what—like this?" Elliot's mouth was inches from hers. Stephanie could feel his warm breath. He covered her mouth with his, and her heart jumped at the contact. His lips were gentle, yet demanding and she was responding to their insistent pressure before she knew it. He pulled back. "Well, it's too late to be afraid of it now; it's happened."

Elliot drew her to him with a powerful movement, kissing her more firmly, passionately, demanding a response to match his own desire. Stephanie struggled against him, trying not to feel the strength of his chest crushed firmly to her breasts, trying to resist the temptation of his lips. The more you let yourself care for him, the farther you let this go, the harder the end will be, warned the inner logical voice that she had always obeyed. She tried to force herself to listen to the logical voice, but after only a moment, her hands were all over his naked back, her fingers exploring the broad shoulders, the tapering waist. Her fingers raked down his chest, and lower to his stomach. Their kisses became more passionate, more demanding of each other. Stephanie's hands moved lower, no longer afraid, and Elliot groaned in response to her searching fingers.

Stephanie's towel lay forgotten at her feet. With a final searching kiss, Elliot released her, and led her, not to the birth below, but to the open air cockpit of the boat.

Stephanie stretched out on the comfortably padded seat opposite the boat's brass wheel and compass. The brass glowed softly in the moonlight. In a moment, Elliot had discarded his shorts and was beside her on

the narrow seat. His hands cupped her breasts gently
as their mouths eagerly found one another.

Stephanie guided Elliot on top of her, and as he
entered her she felt again the motion of her dreams,
felt the rise and fall of the waves, the powerful strength
of the ocean, and the strength of Elliot's body.

When sleep finally came to her that night, Stephanie
was secure in Elliot's arms. Her last thought as sleep
crept over her, was to wonder what happened to the
stars? She knew the answer almost immediately when
she saw the pale streaks of light in the sky, and she
dozed off.

FIFTEEN

Elliot's body sliced through the cool water with sleek grace. He surfaced and shook his wet hair out of his eyes. He drifted upright at the surface, keeping himself afloat with an occasional kick of his strong legs. The *Windy Love* bobbed serenely in the early morning sunlight. From his perspective in the water, she looked like a large, graceful sea bird floating in the bay.

He searched the deck. Still no sign of Stephanie. He'd left her asleep in the cockpit to check on the morning weather and was unable to resist the placid beauty of the water. At first, he'd considered waking her to swim with him, but she looked so peaceful and content he didn't have the heart to disturb her. He knew she'd had little rest since this whole mess began.

Besides that, he had actually been grateful for a little time by himself to sort things out. Last night had been an incredible experience for him. For the first time in thirteen years, he'd experienced the abandon of trusting someone completely. For many years, he'd felt a curtain between his heart and all the other women he'd been with. He'd finally given up trying to raise that

175

curtain. He was used to being alone with his bitterness. It was easier that way.

Then, along came Stephanie Robinson, and she didn't merely raise that curtain, she'd ripped it right down, and the result had been devastating. He'd set out to prove her a fraud, and instead she'd seen through his angry shell with those green eyes and dared him to care about her and her troubles.

He shivered, as the morning coolness of the water began to seep into his bones. He thought of what was ahead. It was Friday morning. Alan Wells, Weston Thomas's managing partner, was expecting Elliot to be in his office Monday morning at 8:00 a.m., with Stephanie in tow. The picture of the old man behind his massive desk was vivid in Elliot's mind. Failure to appear would mean the forfeiture of the performance bond that had been posted, at great cost to the firm, and needless to say, the end of Elliot's career.

Stephanie emerged from the cabin below. She was wearing something that he'd bet was one of his shirts, and her hair was a gorgeous, unbrushed mass that made her look like a beautiful wild animal. She caught sight of him in the water and waved happily. His heart twisted within him at the sight. He waved, and began swimming back with strong, steady strokes. He'd made a promise to her last night; one that he intended to keep.

The sight of Elliot's body cutting strongly through the still waters brought back a flood of warm memories to Stephanie. When the sun awakened her this morning, she'd been distressed to find him gone, but seeing him had instantly calmed her. Now, as she thrilled to the sight of him stroking magnificently back to the boat, she was surrounded by a pleasant haze of images from last night. Elliot's touch had inflamed her with desires and feelings that had never existed for her before. Her skin tingled with the memory of his rough fingers. She bit her lip, and colored slightly as she recalled how she had cried out for him at the end.

He'd promised her that somehow they'd find Leo. She was incredibly grateful for that promise. But this morning, for the first time since this madness started, she was thinking of a time beyond the end of the search. How might things have happened if she and Elliot had met under normal circumstances? Would they have come to love each other? Would they have shared a life?

Wishful thinking, she knew that. For now, she had to be grateful for his promise to see this through, and for what they'd shared. It was pointless to wish for what would never be. At least they had this time together.

Elliot reached the rope ladder and paused at the base of it for a moment. Stephanie noted with delight he hadn't bothered with a swimsuit. She settled herself down on the cockpit bench.

"Avert your eyes, Madam. I'm coming in."

"Whatever do you mean?" Stephanie pretended great innocence. "Just climb right up the ladder."

"Look, Stephanie, I'm buck naked down here, and I figured you wouldn't want me prancing by first thing in the morning."

"On the contrary," said Stephanie stretching out on her stomach and resting her head on her hands, "that is exactly want I want." She waited. Elliot called her bluff, climbing up the ladder with deliberate steps, and rummaging about with elaborate casualness until he found a towel.

Seeing him wet from the sea, in the full glory of the

morning light was even better than the shadowy dusk of last night. He was a beautiful man, magnificently and generously made; and he was hers, if only for a short time.

Elliot wrapped the towel around his waist. "It's still early. We've got time for a quick breakfast before we get underway." He stepped down into the cockpit toward the steps leading to the galley. "What would you like?"

"What I would like," Stephanie said as she leaned out and caught the edge of his towel, "is to skip breakfast." She gently pulled him to her side. She entwined her fingers in his damp hair and pulled his mouth to hers. Their lips met with frantic need.

Elliot slid down beside her on the cockpit seat. She raked her fingers through the cloud of dark curly hair on his chest. Stephanie felt him shiver with anticipation. She rubbed his nipples with her fingertips in a gentle circular motion and watched them tighten into hard, dark peaks. His eyes blazed with captured fire. She felt a sudden surge of satisfaction when she realized that she was the one causing his reaction. She felt the ancient, mystical power of her womanhood within her, the power to please a man that she loved. He worked at the buttons of the shirt she was wearing with trembling fingers, finally popping one off in frustration. Unlike last night, when they had explored each other with the slow movements of a couple who are strangers to one another's bodies, this morning their passion was swift and wildly unrestrained. Their mouths consumed each other greedily. They pleasured each other with confidence. Stephanie helped him with her shirt, and she tossed it aside. A moment later, Elliot's towel had joined it on the floor.

Their union was fast and passionate, and when it

was over they lay together silently for a few minutes, Stephanie's head resting on Elliot's chest.

"Where did you get that scar?" She reached down and gently traced the hard ridge on his knee. For now, at least, his body belonged to her, and she wanted to know its secrets.

"When I was in college, I was in an accident on my motorcycle. I was hit broadside by a delivery van." Elliot's voice was steady, but his eyes were distant and troubled. "I was injured pretty badly. Actually, I was lucky I wasn't killed, although by the time I regained consciousness I wished I had been."

"What made you feel like that?"

He paused a moment and cleared his throat before continuing. "Well, I couldn't play football anymore, of course. That was certainly a part of it. I was going pro after I finished college. An awful lot of my life had been centered around that game. It was almost impossible for me to imagine life without it. But more than that, someone I trusted, had made a lot of plans with—" His voice roughened. "Someone I loved, damn it, decided she couldn't deal with the new me. The No-Longer-A-Big-Football-Hero Elliot McKeon."

"She broke up with you?"

"She didn't even bother with that. She saw me once in the hospital. I never saw her again after that day. Being married to a pathetic victim of fate wasn't in her plans. And she was a woman with plans. I can see that now." His voice hardened. "She left school that semester. I heard later that she'd married a wealthy man, much older." The darkness in his eyes deepened a shade. "I guess she got what she wanted."

Stephanie's heart twisted with sadness for him and anger at the woman who would hurt him so cruelly, but she held back her feelings. She knew instinctively it had been very hard for him to tell her what he had, and she didn't want to step further on his pride with well-meaning sympathies.

"Anyway, after I got out of the hospital and back on my feet, so to speak, I began to take school a whole lot more seriously. I'd been sliding by, with football and all that, so it was an adjustment, but I did it. I turned out to be a pretty good student after all. I finished my undergraduate cum laude, and I was fourth in my class at law school." He laughed shortly. "It's amazing how much time you have to study if you don't practice football and make love to beautiful women." He paused for a moment, then traced her lips delicately with his fingertips. "Guess I'm back in the game on one count anyway."

Stephanie kissed his fingertip gently. "Thank you. For that, you still get breakfast."

When Elliot made the boat ready to head out, Stephanie checked their provisions for breakfast. A few minutes later, Elliot was guiding the *Windy Love* back out to sea while she scrambled eggs in the tiny galley. She found English muffins and jam, but no butter. She toasted the muffins in the oven and made a pot of coffee. As she waited for the coffee to brew, she enjoyed the warm, languid feeling that permeated her whole being. It was the warmth of sharing with someone else. It made preparing a simple meal a supremely satisfying experience.

Stephanie thought of all the meals she'd eaten alone in her life. Broiled chicken on unadorned plates; paper napkins and the television on loud to fill up the empty silence of her tiny kitchen. A couple of times she had tried to make a real meal for herself, with china and a glass of wine. Instead of comforting her, it had only made her feel foolish, and more alone than ever.

By the time she emerged, they were out of the tiny cove. Elliot practically inhaled his breakfast, and praised her cooking highly, which embarrassed her. She knew the truth; she could barely boil water.

After breakfast, Elliot told her his plan. "The coordinates Leo left are about a seven-hour sail from here. The first part should be fairly easy, because we'll be sailing south along the coast, fairly close to shore. We'll be behind the Barrier Reef." He traced their course on the chart, which passed close to many of the off shore islands. "After about five hours, we should reach this break in the Barrier Reef. We'll cut through there to the open ocean. Our destination is another two hours sailing beyond that." He circled an area Stephanie guessed from the scale of the map to be about thirty-six miles off the mainland.

"Logan's Reef?" Stephanie's stomach felt suddenly empty, in spite of breakfast.

"It's an atoll, actually. According to the chart, there's a group of six small islands that fringe the reef of the atoll, although none of them are exactly in the right place to match Leo's directions." Elliot pointed out the locations with his index finger. "The three largest of them are arranged end to end; the two small ones are further along here." He traced the ring of the reef around the atoll. "According to the charts, none of them are inhabited."

They motored for the first hour, but by the middle of the morning a fairly stiff breeze was blowing. Elliot asked Stephanie to hold the wheel on course while he raised the sails.

"Why? Isn't the motor faster?" The idea of raising the sails appealed to her, but seemed contrary to their purpose. They were running out of time.

"Usually. But speed isn't my main concern anyway.

Remember, we're supposed to be pleasure sailors, not a reconnaissance team. We don't want to blow our cover. Under sail, we can keep a lower profile.''

Elliot moved efficiently about the boat, checking the rigging to make sure all lines were correctly arranged. Within a few minutes, the main sail was up, followed by the jib. After Elliot had trimmed them in as close to the wind as he could, he cut the engine. The sails billowed magnificently, the sun turning the soiled canvas to a glistening, pristine white.

Under sail, the *Windy Love* was at her best. Stephanie was thrilled by the feeling of being powered by the wind. When she held the wheel, she felt connected to the fantastic energy source that drove them. Paradoxically, that power was filled with a deep serenity that comforted her. In spite of her uncertainty about what was ahead, she felt herself relaxing under the ministrations of the sun and wind. Soon she stretched out to fully soak up the warmth of the tropical sun.

Elliot stayed at the wheel. Here, along the line of the Barrier Reef, passage would be tricky. Although the reef offered protection, it could be treacherous as well. In some places, the reef was visible just below the surface; in others, the coral heads were hidden, and a careless navigator could run aground. He was a very experienced sailor, and that was exactly why he was being cautious. He knew that the chance of running into trouble in these unfamiliar waters was significant, but he didn't want to burden Stephanie with any additional worries.

She was sitting up now, on the forward area of the deck in front of the cockpit. Her thick hair, glistening in the noon sun, was blown back by the wind, and Elliot's hands remembered its softness brushing across the bare skin of his chest. Her hands were clasped about her knees, and she was staring off toward the mainland, lost in thought. Her hypnotic green eyes were like mysterious, dark pools that challenged a man to dive in and discover their mystery.

Last night he'd taken a challenge. He thought he was safe. He'd been on guard, the old bitterness and pain familiar allies in his fight against being hurt again. He'd thought he could get away. He'd thought he'd be able to taste her sweetness, to drink his fill of her, and then let her go, as he'd always done before. He would be in control. He'd vowed years ago not to be foolish again, and he didn't take the promises he made himself lightly.

But today, as he watched her stretch out her long legs in a graceful gesture that made his throat tighten and turn back to smile at him with lips that begged to be kissed, he knew he'd broken that promise.

SIXTEEN

The opening in the Barrier Reef was marked by a wedge of dramatic, dark blue water spilling in from the open sea. Elliot explained that the passable portion of the opening was much smaller than the dark water made it appear. Stephanie had expected them to sail right through the middle, and in fact, their course appeared to take them that way, but Elliot wasn't satisfied with the angle of their approach. Instead, he brought the boat around and set a course much closer to the left hand side of the opening.

In spite of Elliot's confident handling of the wheel, Stephanie's heart was pounding. The direction they were headed cut very close to the coral heads of the reef on the left. She could see their hard outlines clearly in the lighter water. The seas outside the reef were much rougher than the protected area inside, and swells were breaking over the reef around the opening. The late afternoon trade winds were beginning to blow more strongly. The muscles in Elliot's calves and thighs were tightly bunched as he steadied himself against the motion of the boat, and his mouth was set in a straight hard line. He gave his full attention to guiding her through the pass. Stephanie wrapped her fingers tightly around the cockpit railing and kept her eyes on the passage.

The *Windy Love* sailed through the opening in a graceful burst of motion, right through the center of the dark-blue wedge of water. Stephanie realized Elliot had aimed close to the coral in order to allow for the wind and the current, and that if they'd held their original course, they might have ended up on the reef. She watched him with heightened admiration as he made infinitesimal adjustments to the trim of the sails to compensate for the heavier winds and seas they were sailing into.

There was so much more to Elliot than she'd seen that first morning in her office. Watching him now, moving about the boat with swift assurance, she could hardly imagine him carrying a briefcase and wearing the conservative clothes that had seemed at first meeting to be such a part of him. It was as if he'd shed his cool, controlled, civilized veneer with his professional suits and revealed an earthy, passionate man that lived close to the land and the ocean, not in the rarified atmosphere of corporate law.

The trip to the opening had taken longer than they'd anticipated. It was now late afternoon, but the sky had darkened with clouds, making it appear closer to dusk. Without the sun, the air was growing cool, and Stephanie pulled on a T-shirt. She handed Elliot his shirt and he tugged it over his head. Stephanie watched the intricate interplay of the muscles of his upper body that occurred from the simple action. A brief vision of him emerging naked from the water that morning popped into her head, and she smiled secretly at the memory.

Her smile faded when she noticed the look of concern on Elliot's face.

Elliot peered uneasily at the sky. "I don't like the look of the weather." He scanned the horizon a full three hundred sixty degrees. "We're still a good two hours from Logan's Reef. The only safe anchorage there will be inside the reef of the atoll, and the entrance will be quite a bit smaller than the one we just went through." He ran a big hand through his hair. "If it gets much rougher, or we lose the daylight, we won't be able to make it in the entrance."

Stephanie didn't ask what they would do in that case. The trade winds were really starting to blow now. The wind was kicking up white caps on the water, which now seemed a darker blue. Stephanie went below and changed into jeans and a sweatshirt. When she came back up, the first mist of rain was beginning to hit. A few minutes later, it was coming down in big drops that splattered on the deck.

Elliot fired up the engine. "We'll never make it to Logan's Reef in this weather. It's getting darker all the time." He zipped up the wind breaker Stephanie had brought him. "There's a shallow anchorage at a place called Rock Cay not too much farther. There won't be too much protection, but we've got to get out of the open before this gets any worse." As if in response to his words, a large swell slapped the boat, sending Stephanie sliding off the seat of the cockpit. Elliot caught her in one strong arm and placed her back down. "Hold on. It'll be rough until we get inside."

Rock Cay was ahead. It looked bigger than where they'd anchored last night, but this island didn't have the pretty crescent beach and lush palms. Instead, as its name suggested, it was a rocky ridge rising up from the water, with a shallow indentation of a cove that would offer only minimal shelter. A few scraggly bushes clung tenaciously to the unfriendly land.

The swells were becoming larger, and it seemed to take hours to cover the short distance to Rock Cay. The rain, which had relented for a few minutes, returned with a vengeance, and now was sluicing down in solid sheets.

"Be careful on the deck. Everything will be slippery." Stephanie nodded and clung to the side of the cockpit. "Why don't you go below?" Elliot was shouting now to be heard over the wind and waves. She shook her head strongly. She had no intention of going anywhere without Elliot.

Finally, they were inside the cove. Elliot brought them in to the center of the cove, being careful not to get too close to the island. He dropped the anchor and let out many more yards of line than he had the night before. He grabbed Stephanie's hand and helped her down the steps leading below. "It's batten down the hatches time!" Elliot followed her down the steps and closed the teak hatch behind him. It slammed shut with a bang.

Inside, the sound of the rain was a muffled drumbeat, and the cove protected them from most of the heavy swells. The fading light of the stormy afternoon made the rich teak of the salon glow with a warm brilliance. Stephanie heard a dripping sound and looked around for the source.

"Look at us!" She gestured toward the floor of the salon. They were both soaking wet from the rain and the spray, and a large wet puddle was forming at their feet.

Elliot opened a cupboard and pulled out a stack of thick towels. He put them on the dark wooden table. He unzipped his windbreaker and put it on the table. He pulled Stephanie close to him and gently tugged at the zipper on her sweatshirt. As it came reluctantly down, his knuckles brushed up against Stephanie's nipples, pressing stiffly through the wet fabric of her T-shirt. The unexpected pressure sent electric jolts of pleasure through her. He peeled the sweatshirt off her shoulders. He stopped to admire how the thin, wet fabric clung to her full bosom. He pulled the T-shirt off over her head in a slow languid motion.

A small moan of anticipation escaped Stephanie's lips. A warm inner fire was starting to burn within her, driving away the chill she'd been feeling from the rain. Elliot was working on the zipper to her jeans now, and the feeling of his rough fingers trying to handle the delicate task was incredibly arousing. She helped him slip the wet denim down over her hips, leaving only the tiny wisp of cotton panties in place. Although she was virtually naked, she felt no chill.

Elliot picked up one of the fluffy white towels, and began to gently dry her off, first her face and neck, then moving down to her shoulders and arms, then her breasts. He bent his head down and captured a drop trickling down her right breast with his rough tongue. He moved lower, and her nipple tightened in his mouth. A rough moan of pleasure rose from deep inside her, demanding more. She put her hand on the back of his head and pulled his mouth hard on her breast.

He returned to drying her, moving down her torso, drying her belly, then hooked two fingers through the waist of her panties and pulled them off in a single motion to her feet. She stepped out of them. He dried her thigh, her buttocks, her calves, and finally her feet.

He stood up and stepped back, admiring her like a sculptor might admire his creation. He started to speak, stopped for a moment, and when he spoke again his voice was rough and smokey. "Stephanie," his eyes were dark with emotion, "Let me make love to you."

"No." Elliot looked stricken, but only for a moment. "First I want to dry you." Stephanie smiled, full of feminine mystery.

"Okay." Elliot smiled back. He stood waiting, his hair damp from the rain. A few drops of moisture clung to his jaw line, darkened with a day's beard. Stephanie reached for the edge of his T-shirt. Elliot leaned down so she could peel it off him. She tossed it aside. He had only his cotton shorts on, and they were soaked from the rain. Stephanie ran her hand down his damp chest, flicking the moisture from the trail of dark hair leading to his flat belly, then grabbed the waistband of his shorts and shucked them off in one quick tug. She took two fresh towels from the stack and with one in each hand began to rub him dry with vigorous circular motions, standing on her toes to reach, starting at his neck and shoulders, then moving down the lean planes of his upper body. Elliot shuddered with pleasure as she buffed his torso, then dropped down to rub his thickly muscled legs, starting with his feet and working up to his calves and thighs. When she reached his loins, he bit his lip, but stopped her after only a moment, unable to endure the exquisite pressure. He seized her by her shoulders and pulled her lips to his, crushing their sweetness against his mouth.

They found their way in the dusky light to the bedroom. Elliot stretched Stephanie out on the bed, then covered her throat, her shoulders, her breasts with full, needy kisses that burned her with the contact. She raked her fingers over his back and twisted them in his hair as his searching mouth made a pathway between her breasts and down the soft curve of her stomach. He traced the hollow of her naval with his tongue, then continued lower. She gasped, and cried out as sudden waves of pleasure blurred her vision. A thousand electrical storms played across the inside of her eyelids, and the thunder outside rumbled in answer.

She drew Elliot up to her, brought his lips back to her lips. Her searching fingers kneaded the throbbing muscles of his lower back and buttocks, urging him to take her, now. She wanted him in her.

In one swift stroke, he was joined to her, and their motions together were primal and ancient. She wrapped her legs around him with fierce, aching need. He pressed his mouth over hers with demanding possession. Elliot's mouth explored her ear; her fingers wedged between them to feel the hard ridges of his abdomen. A relentless, sweet struggle of giving and taking.

The storm raged outside, and Stephanie felt its energies flowing into her; the power of the wind, the rain, the sea. All were feeding into her and joining with her to make love to Elliot. Each new peak was matched with more power, more energy at her disposal. As he moved in her, they became part of the power together. The boat pitched and rolled, but she was not afraid. They were a part of it.

Elliot moaned softly, and changed the rhythm of their dance. She urged him on now, faster. She raked her fingers through the damp hair of his chest. Her breath was coming in short gasps. Elliot's scent was all over her and in her now, spicy and warm. His movements within her hit a pinnacle of need and urgency. She reached out to touch him where the muscle of his neck joined his shoulder, and she could feel the spasms of his exploding pleasure there, and in response she dissolved into waves of release, flowing through her like water over parched land.

They lay in the near darkness without speaking, their bodies interlaced together in a jumble of unity. Elliot was softly stroking the small indentation of Stephanie's throat with one long finger, a rhythmic, soothing motion. Stephanie was exploring Elliot's ear with the tip of her little finger.

Gradually, as the storm raged on, they dozed in the darkness. A few hours later, they awoke almost at the same instant, both awakened by something they could not pinpoint.

"Do you hear it?" Elliot's voice was hushed.

"No. What?" Stephanie strained to listen.

"Nothing. It's quiet out there. The storm's gone." His eyes glowed in the darkness. "Tomorrow we're going to Logan's Reef."

Stephanie said nothing, but she reached out and held tight to Elliot as if the storm still raged.

——— SEVENTEEN ———

The morning dawned clear and calm. No sign was left of the storm that had buffeted the *Windy Love* the night before. Elliot checked the boat's rigging for damage while Stephanie made coffee. She brought him a mug as he retied some lines that had pulled loose in the storm. His head was bent over in concentration, and the bright morning sun was pulling brilliant highlights from his glossy dark hair. She put the coffee down beside him and ran her hand through the thick mass. He smiled warmly in response, and gave her a quick kiss on the nose. She sat down next to him and waited for him to finish, scanning the horizon.

A shadowed ring of green and white was floating mirage-like on the deep blue surface to the east. She studied it for a moment before she spoke. "Is that it?" In spite of the warm morning sun, a cold chill fingered the back of her neck.

Elliot looked up from his task and followed her line of vision. "Yes. That's Logan's Reef. With the conditions we've got this morning, we should reach the first island in just over an hour." He wiped his hands on his shirt. "If you're ready, I'd like to get underway."

Stephanie nodded silently. She helped Elliot prepare the boat for sailing. They motored out of the shallow cove of Rock Cay, then raised the sails to catch the brisk trade winds of the early morning. Elliot was silent at the wheel. Stephanie rinsed out their coffee cups in the galley and returned to the cockpit. They didn't speak for a long time, but Stephanie felt it was a good silence, filled with comfortable understanding and tenderness. She wished at that moment that they would never reach their destination, that they might continue as they had for the last two days and nights, sharing talk and making love and absorbing the cleansing warmth of the sun. *It's funny*, Stephanie thought to herself, *in less than a week I've shared more of my life with Elliot than I've shared with people I've known for years. And now, in one way or another, it's all going to be over soon.* A pang of regret cut through her with cold precision. Not for what had passed between them; that she knew she'd cherish for the rest of her life. Her regret was for the future that could never be. A strange image of the two of them on a beach together, watching children playing in the waves flashed briefly through her mind. She pushed it reluctantly away.

Their destination became clearer as they drew nearer. Three islands ran together in a blur of pink and green. Soon, they could discern the nearest island separately from the group. It appeared to Stephanie to be about twice the size of Rock Cay. Unlike where they'd stayed last night, however, this island offered not even a shallow harbor for protection. A narrow beach ran around the perimeter of the island. The vegetation was sparse as well, with only a few coconut palms and scrub bushes covering the interior.

"That's Logan's Cay." Elliot was studying the chart. "The water runs fairly deep right up to the beach, so we can tack in close." Elliot adjusted their course to bring them parallel to the shore line. "There are binoculars in the chart case." Elliot gestured toward the teak box mounted to the right of the cabin steps. Stephanie found the binoculars and handed them to Elliot. He swept the length of the beach slowly several times. "Looks like nobody's been here since Robinson Crusoe." He handed the glasses to Stephanie. "Keep looking. Watch the interior of the island. I'll hold this course until we reach the north end."

Stephanie looked until her eyes ached, but still saw nothing but yards of beach dotted with scraggly sand grass in clumps. The palms were spread far enough apart that she could see through to the sunlight on the other side of the island.

They reached the north end of Logan's Cay without sighting anything but a few sea birds. Elliot kept the boat on a northbound course, although he had to tack farther out as they approached Moon Cay, the next island in the chain.

Moon Cay was distinguished by a very deep, narrow cove, edged with a thick growth of palm trees growing down almost to the water's edge. Through her binoculars, Stephanie spotted a sagging wooden dock at the deepest point of the cove. Elliot didn't enter the narrow cove, but kept heading north. Stephanie kept her eyes trained on the old dock, but there were no signs of activity. Then she caught sight of what looked like the thatched roof of a primitive structure directly back from the dock, mostly obscured by the palms. She pointed it out to Elliot.

"Let's take a closer look." Elliot's tone was even, but Stephanie felt an underlying current of caution. He brought the boat about in a wide smooth arc. "Take the wheel." He gave Stephanie the wheel as he went below for a moment to the utility cabinet beneath the steps. He returned with a flare gun from the emergency kit. He tucked it into the waistband of his jeans and took the wheel back from Stephanie.

They entered the narrow cove still under sail, without starting the engine. The water in the cove was deep and still.

The dock was a rickety looking wooden structure projecting out over the water about fifty feet. The wood pilings and planks were sun bleached to a pale grey. Thick rope hung in heavy lengths from some of the pilings into the water, rotting from the sun and saltwater.

Elliot brought the boat to the end of the dock in a smooth pass, hopped onto the dock and secured the tie lines. Stephanie put the large white rubber bumpers over the side to keep the boat from scraping on the dock.

Elliot gave Stephanie his hand as she stepped onto the dock. The first plank groaned in protest, threatening to give way under her feet. She jumped in fright and grabbed Elliot's arm for support. "Sorry," she admitted in embarrassment, "I guess I'm pretty jumpy."

Elliot put his arm around her. "Don't apologize. You're doing fine." She melted into a powerful bear hug. "Watch your step." Planks were missing in places, and the lagoon was visible in the gaps. They picked their way carefully along the decrepit dock toward the narrow beach.

The thin man put his binoculars down in disgust. "He's got his hands all over her," he muttered to himself. He raised the glasses again. The auburn-haired vixen was clinging to the lawyer's arm now, holding tight as they walked down the dock. Her beautiful hair was blowing back from her face in a cloud, and the thin man thought of twisting it tightly in his fingers. He imagined kissing her full lips. Soon, she would be raking her fingers over his back and crying out, begging him for more, and he would give it to her. He had everything she needed. Stephanie Robinson belonged to him, and it was only a matter of time before she knew it.

He reluctantly turned his gaze to his own dock on Big Cay. No sign yet of Red and Ben. He checked his watch. They would be back soon; he'd taught them to be punctual. He climbed down the tower's narrow ladder carefully and dropped soundlessly to the ground. A small smile played over his lips as he walked briskly back to the main house. It was time to make things ready for Stephanie's arrival.

They reached the narrow beach at the end of the dock. Elliot put his finger to his lips in warning, and they stood quietly on the end of the dock, listening, for a full minute. All Stephanie heard was the gentle lapping of the lagoon on the dock, and the soft groan of the boat rubbing up against the bumpers.

When Elliot seemed satisfied, they started moving toward the large, thatched roof structure hidden in the thick growth of trees ahead. At the edge of the palms was an overgrown path that had once been edged with pink conch shells. Now, only a few remained to mark what looked like once was a wide, well traveled path. The path led to a clearing in the groves. Four large corner posts supported a sharply pitched roof, but there were no walls, only the thatched overhang creating an open-air room. Five mahogany tables and benches were spaced out over the sand floor.

"Looks like a meeting room of some kind." Stephanie touched one of the rough wooden tables.

"Or a group dining room," said Elliot. He bent down and turned upright a bench that was tipped on its side in the sand. A flurry of hundreds of hermit crabs of all sizes poured out of the damp indentation left behind, scrambling madly for new cover. Stephanie watched them in disgust. "Whatever it is, nobody's been here for a long time." Elliot nudged a wayward crab straggling behind with his foot. The crab disappeared into the sand.

Three narrower paths branched off from the clearing, one disappearing straight back toward the far side of the island, the other two heading parallel to the shore line in opposite directions. More broken conch shells bordered the paths sporadically.

They chose the path leading to the left, which veered around the point of the island and back out to the beach. A series of eight thatched roof huts on stilts were scattered down the beach, about fifty feet apart. Tattered remains of hammocks swayed in the breeze.

"This place must have been a resort at one time." Elliot walked to the front of the first cabin and looked up trying to see in. His hand was on the grip of the flare gun.

"A resort?" Stephanie's tone was disbelieving. "It seems awfully primitive."

"Belize isn't a typical tourist destination. It attracts people who want to scuba dive the reef. Plush accommodations aren't an option. By local standards, this would have been a resort."

Elliot made his way up the wooden steps to the first hut's living area. A thick rope served as a handrail up the steps, then wrapped around the narrow veranda. He opened the door slowly, the flare gun drawn. He disappeared inside, then called out the open door.

"Come take a look." Stephanie followed up the

stairs. The interior of the hut was dark, but Elliot propped open one of the thatched windows with a stick. The single room was equipped with two narrow mahogany beds, a rough table, and two straight-back chairs with woven seats. A dirty kerosene lantern was between the beds on a tiny table, its glass globe black with soot.

"Gracious living, Belize-style." Elliot propped open the other two windows, revealing a spectacular view of the lagoon. Stephanie had to admit the place had a primitive charm that was very appealing. Why was it empty now?

They made a quick inspection of the remaining seven huts. All were similarly equipped, although most were in far worse condition than the first one they'd investigated.

"I don't think anyone's been here since the day this place closed down," Elliot said thoughtfully, as they returned on the path back to the clearing and the dining hall.

"What do you suppose happened?" Stephanie felt a strange sense of regret over the lost resort, as if it were a beloved destination of her own that she'd found so changed. The feeling reminded her of a visit to her grandmother's house several years after her grandmother's death. Even though much about the place was unchanged, the house she'd remembered had been lost forever to time.

"A couple of bad seasons, maybe. Maybe a storm did damage the owner couldn't afford to repair. It looks as if they just packed up and left one day."

The dappled sunlight and shadow of the path gave way to the brightness of the clearing. They next investigated the short path that led directly back from the clearing. It ended at a small open-air enclosure, a miniature version of the dining hall, covering a rusting piece of machinery. Vines with bright purple flowers were growing over it, as if to conceal it, to hide the unnatural intrusion of man's technology in the island paradise.

"Air compressor. Diesel from the smell." Elliot circled the ancient hulk. "There's even fuel left." Elliot kicked at one of the rusty five-gallon cans stacked against a tree behind the machine. Stephanie's stomach lurched as she recalled the long moments of panic in the compressor room in George Town. She was grateful to return back to the clearing.

The last remaining path took them to the beach on the other side of the island. The next adjacent island, Big Cay, looked close enough to swim to. They continued walking down the beach until they reached a sand spit that projected out into the narrow channel between Moon Cay and Big Cay. The ocean currents had built the sand up high enough to create a natural bridge between the two islands. The water appeared to be no deeper than two feet at the middle point.

They stood in silence for a moment, staring across the channel to Big Cay, past the point where the two islands nearly connected was a small, perfect beach. Nestled in the palms bordering the beach was a structure, similar in design and construction to the huts on Moon Cay, but much larger. A wide veranda commanded a sweeping view of the lagoon.

"What's that?" Stephanie felt her pulse quickening.

"Probably the owner's house. He would have lived here year round, so he probably needed a few more comforts than the guests." Elliot touched the flare gun briefly. "I'd better take a look."

Stephanie nodded mutely. She'd felt no fear on the island so far, only a vague sense of uneasiness. But now, facing the house on Big Cay, she felt the icy clutch of fear at her spine. She tried to shake it off, unsuccessfully. She grabbed Elliot's hand firmly. "Let's go."

They crossed the sand spit easily, their sneakers protecting their feet from the rough coral projecting through the coarse sand. Once on the Big Cay side, they scrambled over the small incline to the beach where the big house waited.

The house appeared as deserted and decaying as the huts on the other island. Thick wooden shutters concealed the open-air windows, and several of the slats were missing. The mahogany lounge furniture on the veranda was broken and sunbleached.

Elliot led them cautiously toward the house, staying on the side as they approached, avoiding the shuttered windows facing the water. They reached the stairs running up the side of the house from the beach to the veranda and the front door.

"You stay out here. I'm going in to take a look." Elliot pulled the flare gun from his waist.

"No. I'll go with you." Stephanie's eyes told him there was no point in arguing.

Elliot squeezed her hand firmly, and she saw respect reflected in his eyes. "Okay, but stay behind me until we get our bearings." They proceeded up the stairs in silence. The wide veranda looked relatively solid, but they were careful as they approached the door. Elliot stopped outside the door and listened for a moment, then opened it with a strong push.

The light from the door revealed a living room furnished with the same kind of wooden furniture they'd seen in the guest huts. Rough finished shelves covered one whole wall, filled with hundreds of books. Two doors led to other rooms in the rear of the house. One was closed, the other slightly ajar.

Stephanie's heart was racing. Something was very wrong. This room didn't feel like the huts on Moon Cay. In spite of the shuttered windows, the air was fresh, not musty. She realized in a flash the veranda outside had been swept clean of sand. An ashtray on the coffee table overflowed with cigarette butts. A book was open beside it. This house was being lived in.

Elliot looked at her and she saw the same conclusion in his cool, determined eyes. A soft, scraping sound came from beyond the closed door. Elliot approached the door, holding the flare gun barrel up in his right hand. He opened and entered the door in one strong movement.

There was a moment of silence that seemed to last an eternity, followed by the sound of Elliot swearing softly. Stephanie was through the door in an instant. She bit back a scream of surprise and terror.

On the floor of the bedroom, bound with nautical lines and electrical tape, was Leo Martindale. His face was covered with a scraggly beard, and his grey hair was matted and filthy. His eyes were open, but glazed with fatigue. He looked at them without recognition.

Elliot propped him upright and removed the tape from his lips and pulled out the grimy handkerchief that was stuffed in his mouth. "Oh, my God, Leo, are you alright?" Stephanie studied his face. His eyes didn't acknowledge her at first, then suddenly a dim light seemed to turn on inside of him.

"Stephanie? . . . I tried to . . . Stephanie." He smiled slightly and his eyes drifted shut. Elliot was working on releasing the knots around Leo's hands, so Stephanie struggled with the ropes at his ankles. Elliot freed Leo's hands, and took over from Stephanie. In a few minutes, they had him free. Leo opened his eyes and this time seemed more alert.

"Leo, what happened? Who did this to you?" Stephanie didn't notice the hot tears running down her cheeks at first. She wiped them away roughly with the backs of her hands.

"Stephanie, there's no time for questions now." Elliot's controlled voice was like cold steel. "We've got to get him back to the boat." Elliot stood and started to bring Leo to his feet. "Come on, it's not far. I can carry you if you can't walk." Elliot looped Leo's arm over his neck. Stephanie took Leo's other side and gently walked him to the other room. Leo was staggering under the effort of walking. "I think I'd better carry him, or we'll never get back to the boat." Elliot lifted Leo off his feet smoothly.

A sharp crack interrupted them as the front door of the house was kicked open. Stephanie's throat closed on a scream as the two men who had attacked her at Leo's place burst through the door. The big, red-haired giant held a gun in his hand, which he swept threateningly over the three of them. The two stepped aside silently, one on each side of the door, to let a third man step in between them.

A tall, thin man wearing thick glasses stepped delicately into the room. His sandy hair was cut very short over a large, oddly-shaped head, and he was neatly dressed in pressed chinos and a long sleeve button-down shirt. He was strangely familiar to Stephanie, and a part of her mind was clicking madly, struggling to make the connection.

His thin lips quivered with some hidden pleasure, and his pale gaze fixed on her as if they were alone together, sharing some private moment. He waved his delicate, bony hands in an expansive gesture of greeting.

"Welcome to my island, Stephanie. I've been expecting you. I'm certain you will enjoy it here."

EIGHTEEN

The thin man's high-pitched, reedy voice brought the memory of a dozen unpleasant conversations rushing back to Stephanie. She'd met Oliver Lodfuss in person only a handful of times, but her frequent phone conversations with him made her skin crawl. She'd always thought Oliver to be the perfect image of the rich man's ineffectual son, with no trace of the gritty work ethic and shrewd mind with which his father had built an empire. At forty, he was little more than his father's lackey, doing tasks too menial for his father's more competent employees.

"Ben will take care of that flare for you, Mr. McKeon." Oliver Lodfuss acknowledged Elliot for the first time, his pale hazel eyes flicking over him with distaste. Ben pulled the flare gun from Elliot's jeans. "Put Martindale down there." Lodfuss gestured toward the dirty couch. Elliot lowered Leo's limp body to a sitting position.

"Who are you?" Elliot's voice was even, but Stephanie heard a roughness tearing away at the control. Elliot's cobalt eyes blazed with menace. A vein was beating a strong pulse in the side of his neck. His right hand clenched and unclenched in the same rhythm. The red-haired man with the gun took a menacing step in Elliot's direction.

Lodfuss raised an eyebrow. "I'm terribly sorry, I didn't mean to be rude. I'm Oliver Lodfuss. Stephanie and I are old, dear friends, aren't we?" Stephanie felt his leering gaze trail over her body like a slimy hand. She'd been fending off Oliver Lodfuss since her first year at Martindale and Associates. When he first visited the office with his father, he limited himself to staring at her body, but on the phone he became more direct. Something about the anonymity of the phone made him bold, and every conversation included many compliments on her appearance, and an invitation for drinks, for dinner, for a movie. The more Stephanie politely declined, the more insistent he'd become, until she'd finally told him bluntly that she had absolutely no interest in going out with him. After that, he had never come to the office again, conducting all his business by phone, and their conversations took a different, almost sinister tone. He'd be strictly business throughout, but Stephanie felt a dark, unspoken innuendo in his words that disturbed her more than his open advances had. Several times she'd almost mentioned it to Leo, but had decided it was her own problem to solve.

"Oliver, is your father behind this whole scheme?" Stephanie fought to keep the fear out of her voice.

"My father has nothing to do with any of this!" Oliver Lodfuss's voice cracked. "This is mine, all mine! I don't need him, and I don't need his money. I've got more money now than that old tightwad ever made in his whole life!" His eyes crackled with angry brilliance. "Everybody thinks my father is such a smart businessman. Well, he's nothing but a bull-headed old fool who got lucky. No matter what the old man says, I'm the one with the brains!" His eyes softened slightly. "But you knew that all along, didn't you, Stephanie?" His voice became deathly calm again. "You were just waiting for me to prove myself, so I could be worthy of you. You won't have to wait much longer. I've got everything you need." His bony hands caressed the air delicately. "We're going to be very happy together." He licked his thin lips with a pink tongue. "I'm going to share everything I have with you."

Revulsion fought with fear in Stephanie's stomach. At that moment, Leo stirred and spoke from the couch. "Get away, Stephanie. He'll hurt you." His tongue was thick from fatigue. His eyes suddenly focused sharply. "He's crazy."

Oliver Lodfuss shrieked sharply, and rushed forward like a predatory bird. He raised his hand and struck Leo sharply across the face. Elliot dove for Lodfuss's knees, tackling him to the floor in one swift move and pinning Lodfuss' spindly body beneath his massive torso.

The red-haired man moved with surprising agility, and his burly arms encircled Stephanie before she could react. One arm wrapped her chest like steel bands, while the free arm pressed the cold steel of the gun barrel against her temple.

"Get off 'im, or the lady dies." The Cockney twang was harsh in her ear. His breath reeked of rum. "Help him decide, Ben." The Carib stood menacingly over Elliot. Leo was slumped over on the couch, his eyes closed.

Elliot's eyes burned over Stephanie as he sat slowly back on his knees. Ben grabbed one of Elliot's arms and twisted it behind his back and pulled him to his feet with a wrenching jerk.

Oliver Lodfuss got to his feet gingerly, moving his limbs experimentally, checking for damage. "That was quite rude, Mr. McKeon. And really quite stupid." He turned toward Stephanie. "Let her go, Red. Can't you see you are frightening her?" Red released Stephanie; she stepped away and her hand flew involuntarily to the spot on the side of her head where the gun's barrel had pressed its cold kiss. Lodfuss reached out and touched her arm in consolation. "I'm terribly sorry, Stephanie." Her skin shivered under his dry, cool fingers. "We'll get this unpleasantness over with soon."

"Don't touch her." Elliot's voice was filled with coiled menace.

"Or what?" Lodfuss asked mildly. "You'll try another brave football tackle?" He broke into a high-pitched, shrill laugh that raked like knives down Stephanie's back. Still laughing, he pulled a large book from the bookcase and extracted a small revolver from the space behind it. The laugh faded, and Lodfuss was instantly composed again. "That would be very foolish, Mr. McKeon." His voice was mild again. "Ben, Red, let's escort our guests back to their boat." Lodfuss snaked his arm around her waist. "Lead the way, dearest." His other hand held the small gun casually, delicately, as if it were a glass of wine.

Stephanie looked silently to Elliot. What should she do? Red had his gun planted squarely in the middle of Elliot's back. A wrong move and Elliot would be dead instantly. Elliot nodded to her, almost imperceptibly.

"The boat's on the other island." Stephanie's throat was so tightly constricted she was amazed to hear words come out of it.

Lodfuss steered her through the front door and down

the steps. "I'm well aware of where the *Windy Love* is." Stephanie was startled to hear him use the name. Ben followed down the steps, half-carrying, half-dragging Leo. His eyes were open, and he appeared to be regaining full consciousness. Stephanie's heart was torn apart within her. He looked awful. What horrible things had he endured?

Next to the last down the steps of the house was Elliot, with Red menacingly close behind him. His steps were sure and proud. Stephanie's regret surged through her veins like a deadly venom. Elliot was here because of her. Hot tears formed behind her eyes, but remained unreleased. She loved him, and now it was all over. Not the way she had thought it would end, but in another, far darker destruction. Their eyes met for a brief moment, and in translucent cobalt depths she saw a vision of the two of them, walking together on a beach. Her throat ached with unshed tears.

They made their way down the beach in front of the house to the sand spit. Oliver Lodfuss chatted pleasantly away to her, proudly showing off the island. He kept his left arm wrapped around her waist, while he gestured with the gun in his other hand. They walked about ten yards ahead of the others. Stephanie longed to look back to Elliot, to call out to him, but she was afraid of upsetting Lodfuss.

"This was quite a popular spot with a very small, select group of travellers in the '60's and '70's. The resort fell on hard times in the last decade, and the owner lost the islands to the bank." He lowered his voice conspiratorially. "I was able to pick it up for a song several years ago."

"You've owned this place for years?" The horror of the situation couldn't keep her from trying to understand what had happened.

"Yes, I bought it with a little bit of money my mother left me when she died." His thin lips twisted. "And that was her own money to give me freely—it had nothing to do with the old man." He wrinkled his nose in disgust. "I bought it under an assumed name. No one else knows about it." His tone became intimate and confiding. "I wanted it for a special reason." He looked at Stephanie, his eyes tracing the features of her face slowly, then slipping gradually down her body. "Do you know what that reason was?"

She shook her head, unable to speak, afraid of the answer.

"I wanted a place where you and I could always be alone together." They stopped at the edge of the sand spit. His pale eyes were enormous behind his thick glasses. "I love you, Stephanie. I have from the first moment I met you. And someday, you'll love me, too. I am sure you will." He ran a cool dry finger down the side of her throat. "We'll have lots of time together, I promise."

Ben and Leo, and Red and Elliot caught up with them at the water's edge. Lodfuss gestured the others ahead, and he and Stephanie followed behind. Stephanie noted that in spite of the casual way he handled the gun, he was watching the four men in front carefully. She knew with a chilling certainty that Oliver Lodfuss had invested too much in this sick fantasy to be careless now.

They reached the clearing where the dining hall stood. Lodfuss gestured Leo and Elliot to one of the wooden benches. "Sit down." Leo seemed fully conscious now, his eyes wide with fear. Elliot was silent, but Stephanie could see his mind working at a breakneck pace.

Red and Ben disappeared down the short path toward

the compressor. They returned in less than three minutes, each carrying two five-gallon drums of diesel fuel. "To the dock, gentlemen." Lodfuss waved Elliot and Leo toward the path leading back to the dock; Ben and Red trailed behind with the fuel. Red still had his gun shoved in his waistband; likewise, Ben was carrying the flare gun he'd taken from Elliot. Lodfuss kept his left arm tightly around Stephanie's waist as they followed.

They reached the beach. The *Windy Love* bobbed serenely at the end of the dock, a glistening vision of clean white fiberglass and dark gleaming teak. Lodfuss stopped as Ben and Red put down the fuel. Red drew his gun and motioned Elliot and Leo down the dock.

"Perhaps you and I should stay here. We can see just as well right here from the beach." Lodfuss' voice was bright and cheerful, as though they were waiting for a parade to pass by.

Stephanie watched in horror as Red and Ben shoved Leo and Elliot down the dock to the boat. While Red kept his revolver carefully aimed at Elliot's head, they bound Leo's hands and feet with lines from the rigging and dumped him in the cockpit. Keeping the gun at Elliot's temple, they tied him tightly and dropped him alongside Leo. Even from the distance of the beach, Stephanie heard the heavy thud of Elliot hitting the bottom of the cockpit. They were out of her sight completely now, below her line of vision.

Red and Ben returned to the dock for the cans of diesel fuel. They unscrewed the caps and began methodically soaking the *Windy Love* from stem to stern in fuel. Fuel sloshed over the sails, sending dark stains over the white surface. A dark slick was forming in a circle on the lagoon around the boat, spreading in concentric, oily rings.

Stephanie wanted to look away, wanted to tear her eyes from the sight she knew was coming, but she seemed to have been turned into stone. She couldn't turn her head. She could no longer feel the pressure of Lodfuss's fingers digging into the flesh of her side. It was as if a hateful kind of second sight had descended upon her; she could see the future, and was powerless to change it.

The two men finished with the fuel, and flung the empty cans into the cockpit, where they landed with a hollow metallic ring. Ben cast off the forward line, and untied the aft line and looped it twice around the dock's corner piling. The *Windy Love* began to drift nose out into the lagoon, held only by the single line. Red hopped on board and scrambled to the cockpit. The engine started with a roar. He pushed the throttle open and the boat strained forward. He spun the wheel to the left, and in three quick steps was back on the dock. Ben released the line and the boat motored powerfully out into the deep waters of the lagoon.

Ben took aim with the flare gun and fired. One, two, three flaming missiles landed, and the boat caught fire. Deceptively slow at first, the fire licked lasciviously around the edges of the deck, prolonging its pleasure. Billowing dark smoke completely obscured the boat and the acrid smell of melting fiberglass filled the air. When the fire reached the sails, a solid wall of flame jumped the length of the boat. Stephanie felt the heat against her face, and she wished it were hot enough to sear her eyes blind so she couldn't continue to watch.

Red and Ben retreated back to the beach to watch the end of their handiwork. A moment later, the gas tank of the boat exploded, scattering molten fiberglass and ash over the surface of the lagoon. Mercifully, at that same moment, Stephanie was able to close her eyes to shut out the nightmare, but the image burned through her closed lids anyway. She felt her heart sear with a pain so deep and ripping that she knew she would welcome death if it meant the end of the pain.

When she finally opened her eyes, she wasn't dead. She was on her hands and knees, her hands splayed out against the coarse sand. Oliver Lodfuss was standing a few steps in front of her, watching the remains of the wreckage burn down to nothing on the water. Red and Ben stood at the base of the dock. The incredible pain that was within her was transformed into icy hate and rage, and she thought in an instant she would be on Lodfuss, tearing out his hair and ripping at his eyes with her nails. But although she commanded her body to move, it didn't respond, and so she was still on her knees when Oliver Lodfuss raised the small revolver and put a bullet neatly in the back of Ben's skull, and another in Red's forehead as he turned around with a surprised expression on his face.

She was still on her knees when he turned around and walked to her. Lodfuss pulled her to her feet, gently but firmly. "Now it's just the two of us, darling. You needn't be frightened any longer. We're all alone now." He reached out and stroked her hair slowly. She stepped back in revulsion and fear. Her grief over Elliot had formed into a steely mass of hatred. She could not—would not let him win. She would fight lies with lies. Madness with madness.

"You're a fool." Stephanie spat out the words with all the anger and hatred and pain inside her. Lodfuss looked shocked. She seized on his surprise. "It's over, Oliver."

"What are you talking about?" His pasty white face blanched even paler. Sunlight glinted off his glasses.

"All the money! It's already been found. How long

do you think it took the authorities to find the secret accounts in Cayman, and in Switzerland, too?'' She could tell her brazen lies were striking close to secret fears he carried deep within himself. Beads of sweat were forming on Lodfuss's forehead and running down his face.

"That's impossible. I used Martindale's own passwords. They would never be able to trace the money. And now that Martindale's gone, of course they'll think he was the one responsible.'' His voice betrayed the fears he'd never spoken. "Stephanie, we have everything! We'll be happy here together, forever!'' He took an uncertain step forward, as if to embrace her. Stephanie jumped out of reach.

"The international authorities have already confiscated all the funds. You're a complete failure! You can never have me! I despise failure!'' Stephanie shrieked her last words and bolted down the beach. Lodfuss's shock lasted only long enough for Stephanie to get a few yards' lead down the beach before she heard his footsteps close behind her. Her long legs pumped, but the sand was soft and gave way under her feet.

Her left foot slipped on a clump of beach grass, and she hit the sand hard and rolled down a small incline. She clawed desperately at the slipping sand, struggling to stand and run. She looked back to see Lodfuss coming over the incline toward her, his face a murderous mask of anger. Somehow, she got to her feet for a few more steps before she tripped and fell again, hitting her head sharply against the ground. Her face was in the gritty sand as Lodfuss's shrill scream of surprise ripped through her consciousness.

Elliot's cheek beat with a pulse of pain against the rough surface of the fiberglass deck. The smell of diesel fuel was overpowering in the cockpit. He could see Leo's bound feet twisted at a cruel angle projecting out from behind the base of the wheel. The roar of the engine beneath the deck labored as the boat pulled powerfully against the one line restraining it.

Elliot twisted his hands against the thick rope loops that bound them behind his back. The rough line tore the skin away from his knuckles as he wrenched his right hand free of the restraint. Being careful to stay low on the floor of the cockpit, he quickly released his left hand and went to work on his ankles. Ben had done a better job on the knots there, and sweat poured into Elliot's eyes as he struggled with the line. The few seconds it took him to untie his ankles passed like hours.

Elliot crawled over to Leo, who although conscious, appeared to be deep in shock. His open eyes were bleary with fear and fatigue. Elliot's strong fingers worked with frantic precision on the knots at Leo's ankles and wrists.

The *Windy Love* surged powerfully out into the waters of the deep lagoon, released from its restraining line. With a shrill hiss, a flare landed on the deck to the right of the cockpit. Flames ran along the deck toward the cockpit. As Elliot finished with the final knot at Leo's ankles, the second and third flares hit the deck. Thick, black smoke billowed around the boat, enveloping it in a dense oily cloud.

Elliot hooked Leo's left arm over his neck and stood up, unable to see through the acrid smoke. He pulled Leo's limp body upright, and stepped up over the side of the cockpit away from shore. Holding Leo tightly to him, Elliot jumped over the side into the dense cloud. As they hit the water, the sail caught fire behind them.

Elliot could feel the blast of the heat even as they plunged beneath the cool surface of the lagoon.

When she lifted her face from the sand and turned back toward Lodfuss, Stephanie thought she was already dead. No, she was hallucinating, because she clearly saw Elliot, shimmering wet, only inches from Lodfuss. His body flew out in a lean arc, catching Lodfuss at the waist. His knee was in the middle of his back, his big hands pushing Lodfuss's face into the sand, pinning his thin arms behind him. But in a moment, Stephanie knew, the hallucination would be over, and Lodfuss would be on top of her.

But the hallucination not only continued, it spoke to her. "Stephanie! Get his gun! He dropped it back down the beach a few yards." Stephanie got to her feet and ran back toward the dock. She found the gun in the sand and gave it to the hallucination. Her hand brushed his as she gave it to him and it was solid flesh. "Go check on Leo. He's back on the dock. And see if you can find any line." Stephanie nodded mutely and ran back to the dock, wanting desperately to believe the impossible. Don't think, she told herself. Don't think, just act. Keep it going, keep the illusion real.

She saw the bodies of Red and Ben sprawled on the sand, the water of the lagoon splashing gently at their feet. She gave them a wide berth, suddenly fearful they might spring up to clutch at her legs.

Leo was stretched out on the wood, soaking wet, coughing and wheezing, but definitely alive. She went to his side and laid her hand across his forehead. Definitely not a hallucination.

"Leo, just hold on. You'll be okay." His eyes were open, and he seemed to hear her. She squeezed his hand firmly. She was relieved to feel a slight pressure in return. Satisfied Leo was alright for the moment, she found a length of rope at the end of the dock; one of the *Windy Love*'s docking lines. She untied it and brought it back to Elliot. Lodfuss was sobbing uncontrollably into the sand. "Failure . . . all my plans . . . failure." He offered no resistance as Elliot tied his wrists together with an expert knot, then his feet. Only then did he rise from his position on top of Lodfuss.

Elliot's lips crushed against hers in a riot of sweet sensations, too real to be a dream. His arms drew her into a haven of strength and safety. She laid her head against his chest and heard the beating of his heart and the passage of his breath before she dared to speak. She ran her fingers over him, searching his solidity. He was real. He was alive. "Elliot, you're alright, dear God, what happened? I saw the boat, and the fire and—" Elliot hushed her.

"Don't talk right now. Everything will be all right," he murmured, stroking her head soothingly, cradling it gently against his solid shoulder.

"I had myself untied before Red and Ben released the boat. I think they were nervous about the fire, so they didn't take time to tie us securely. I got Leo free, and we stayed down on the floor of the cockpit until the smoke was thick enough to cover us from shore. We jumped into the water on the opposite side and swam as far out as we could. We found a coral outcropping to hold on to until after the gas tank blew. It was pretty rough on Leo; I had to carry him almost the whole way." He paused for a moment. "All I could think about was you alone here with Lodfuss. I had to get back."

Stephanie felt the pounding of her heart beating against Elliot's chest, and it seemed to be growing stronger until she thought she could actually hear it.

She lifted her head in confusion. It wasn't her heart. The sound was growing louder still.

The helicopter appeared in the distance, flying directly toward the island. The beating noise of the blades grew nearer, until the helicopter was hovering over the surface of the lagoon, blowing away all traces of the column of black smoke from the burning boat, and disturbing the surface of the water into a white froth as it settled gently down.

Stephanie closed the thick file on her desk and looked wearily at her watch. Seven o'clock already, and she still had several hours of work ahead. She stretched out her legs and kicked her shoes off under her desk. She padded in her stocking feet down the hall to the coffee pot. The office was dark and silent, everyone else already gone for the day. Fortunately, she'd been able to reassemble almost the entire original staff without too much trouble. Leo's office was dark as well. Good; Stephanie had taken it as her personal responsibility to make sure he worked as few hours as possible for the next month. Although, fortunately, he'd come through the kidnapping without any serious physical injuries, the doctor had warned him that the stress and fatigue had taken a serious toll on him. He needed to take it easy.

Sounds like good advice, she thought ironically, as she returned to her desk. She hadn't been home before 9:00 p.m. once since she'd returned to California two weeks ago. Contacting employees, straightening out customer accounts, and meeting with Detective Simms and other officials had occupied every minute of Stephanie's time. The endless amount of each day's work had been a welcome distraction from the memories of Elliot she was trying to put behind her. The nights alone had been harder. She was back home now, in the real world, and it was time to get back to normal. Yet, in spite of her efforts, at the busiest times of the day, an evocative image of him would intrude into her mind, sending her into a spinning whirlwind of feeling, and no amount of concentration could banish it.

She hadn't seen Elliot since he'd said good-bye to the two of them at the airport in Belize City. She and Leo were returning home to Newport Beach, while Elliot was flying to George Town to meet with the international banking officials in Cayman to arrange for the release of the embezzled funds. Elliot hugged her tight to him and kissed her once, a sweet lingering farewell that mixed desire and resignation. Her heart had twisted painfully within her in response to that silent message. Then he shook Leo's hand. "Take care of her," he said solemnly.

Stephanie sipped the stale coffee without tasting it. She wasn't sure when Elliot had arrived back in California, but she hadn't heard from him. At least he could have taken the time to call and let her know he was safely back home. She took the next customer file from the stack on her credenza and tried to concentrate on her work. A persistent memory of Elliot at the wheel of the *Windy Love*, his sculpted chest glistening dark bronze in the tropical sun and the wind tousling his hair, was weaving into her thoughts. The memory brought a warm glow, followed by a cold stab of loss. She had fallen in love with Elliot. She had known from the very instant her feelings had started to awaken that their time together would end as suddenly as it had begun, yet that knowledge had been a slim comfort to her. She simply missed being with him, missed the way he made her feel, missed the sense of sharing that had marked their days on the boat. It was like she had discovered a long-missing piece of herself, only to have it snatched cruelly away at the moment of discovery. She closed her eyes and rubbed the bridge of her nose between thumb and forefinger. Maybe she should go home and get some sleep. She could come in early tomorrow. She wasn't getting any work done tonight anyway.

Elliot stood quietly in the darkness of the outer office. The heavy oak door closed silently behind him. Stephanie's light was on and her door was open. From his position by the receptionist's desk, he could see the top of her head curled down in concentration. Her hair was pulled back in a neat French braid. He liked it better down. A rush of sensation swept over him as he remembered the dark lilac essence that exuded from it when she let it go free. He remembered the feel of the thick tresses in his fingers and the tingling way it swept over his bare chest.

He hadn't been able to get her out of his mind. Oh, he'd been plenty busy alright. It seemed as if every minute since they'd gotten off Logan's Reef had been filled with meetings, negotiations, and travel. Although Oliver Lodfuss's confession had cut short the investigation by the local authorities, and he had been returned under custody to the U.S., that had just been the beginning. He'd had to deal with both Belize and Cayman authorities in the matter of the shootings of Red and Ben, and then the real work had begun on the verification of Lodfuss's connection to the missing funds. Through it all, he'd shielded Stephanie from as much of the scrutiny as he could, trying to focus the attention on himself and away from her. She'd suffered far too much in this already. He intended to make sure she didn't have to suffer anymore.

"Hello, Ms. Robinson." Stephanie looked up, startled, into the deep cobalt eyes that had dominated her thoughts, sleeping and waking, for the past two weeks. Elliot was standing in the doorway to her office, his big frame casually propped against one side. He was wearing a dark navy suit and a bright yellow tie, and she flashed back to that early morning when she had first seen him. She felt his gaze sear over her as she had that first time, but this time the fire burning in his eyes was lit from another source. There were little lines around his mouth that softened it in a way that made her want to smooth them away with her kisses.

"Hello." She wanted to speak, to say something clever to pass the awkward moment by, but the words weren't coming. Her response to Elliot was immediate and visceral. Two weeks apart hadn't dimmed the strong reaction of her body to his; indeed, it had intensified it. The warm flush of response to his essential maleness was growing within her. Her throat constricted and her breath was coming faster. She found her voice.

"When did you finally make it back home? Are things getting back to normal?" She intended her tone to be light and conversational, but her voice betrayed her, coming out strained and husky. She got up from her chair and walked to the side of her desk. Her knees felt dangerously weak beneath her. "I was beginning to wonder if I was ever going to see you again." Elliot remained in the doorway.

"I just got back this morning. I believe we have some unfinished business to attend to." His deep baritone was rough with some emotion she couldn't read.

"I see. And what is that?" She felt her heart beating an impossible rhythm, a fierce tattoo of hope and fear.

"I believe you agreed to go on a rather important trip with me that was unfortunately cut short. I would like to complete that trip."

"I would think you've probably had enough of traveling with me, Mr. McKeon. What trip are you referring to?"

"Our honeymoon."

Elliot was beside her in two big steps, drawing her into the solid circle of his body, his mouth seeking hers with a need that went beyond desire, crushing her lips against his. Stephanie felt the flush explode within her in a spectacular burst of energy spreading a glow of warmth from the center of her chest in rings throughout her body.

"Stephanie, I need you. I have to be with you." His hands held her gently by her shoulders, the warmth of his hands warming the skin under the fabric of her blouse. He studied her face with tender attention before he continued. "I love you, Stephanie. Please marry me."

Stephanie's eyes locked Elliot's. For a long moment the two of them existed in a separate world.

"I love you, Elliot. And yes, I will." Her answer came from deep within her soul, unfettered by logical thought. Their lips found each other again in a union of passion and tenderness. Her soft curves melded together pliantly to the hard planes of his body. Elliot's hands worked gently at her French braid, and her hair came down, surrounding them in a cloud of lilac that blended with Elliot's warm, spicy essence.

Elliot pulled back from her achingly tender mouth.

"I want to hear you say it again."

"Yes."

"Again."

"Yes."

"Again."

Stephanie put one hand on the back of his head and drew his mouth to an inch away from hers. "Yes. Yes. Yes," she said softly, then let their mouths meld together.

Her hands traveled over his broad back, revelling in the coiled power and strength of the man, the man who had saved her life more than once. Years of stored-up tenderness and passion were flowing from Elliot to her, through his eyes, his hands, his mouth, breaking through the hard shell of bitterness that had sealed off his heart for so long, and Stephanie knew with a sudden certainty that, in a way, she had saved his life as well.

Two lives nearly lost, and found again in one another. She smiled to herself at the natural symmetry of it, then let the thought go in the flood of sensations flowing back and forth between them in an endless, powerful tide.